PENGUIN CLASSICS
Inspector Cadaver

T0200796

'I love reading Simenon. He makes me think of Chekhov'
– William Faulkner

'A truly wonderful writer . . . marvellously readable – lucid, simple, absolutely in tune with the world he creates'
– Muriel Spark

'Few writers have ever conveyed with such a sure touch, the bleakness of human life'   – A. N. Wilson

'One of the greatest writers of the twentieth century . . . Simenon was unequalled at making us look inside, though the ability was masked by his brilliance at absorbing us obsessively in his stories'   – *Guardian*

'A novelist who entered his fictional world as if he were part of it'   – Peter Ackroyd

'The greatest of all, the most genuine novelist we have had in literature'   – André Gide

'Superb . . . The most addictive of writers . . . A unique teller of tales'   – *Observer*

'The mysteries of the human personality are revealed in all their disconcerting complexity'   – Anita Brookner

'A writer who, more than any other crime novelist, combined a high literary reputation with popular appeal'   – P. D. James

'A supreme writer . . . Unforgettable vividness'   – *Independent*

'Compelling, remorseless, brilliant'   – John Gray

'Extraordinary masterpieces of the twentieth century'
– John Banville

ABOUT THE AUTHOR

Georges Simenon was born on 12 February 1903 in Liège, Belgium, and died in 1989 in Lausanne, Switzerland, where he had lived for the latter part of his life. Between 1931 and 1972 he published seventy-five novels and twenty-eight short stories featuring Inspector Maigret.

Simenon always resisted identifying himself with his famous literary character, but acknowledged that they shared an important characteristic:

> My motto, to the extent that I have one, has been noted often enough, and I've always conformed to it. It's the one I've given to old Maigret, who resembles me in certain points . . . 'understand and judge not'.

Penguin is publishing the entire series of Maigret novels.

GEORGES SIMENON

Inspector Cadaver

Translated by WILLIAM HOBSON

PENGUIN BOOKS

PENGUIN CLASSICS

UK | USA | Canada | Ireland | Australia
India | New Zealand | South Africa

Penguin Books is part of the Penguin Random House group of companies
whose addresses can be found at global.penguinrandomhouse.com.

First published in French as *L'Inspecteur Cadavre* by Éditions Gallimard 1944
This translation first published 2015

010

Set in Dante MT Std 12.5/15 pt
Typeset by Palimpsest Book Production Limited, Falkirk, Stirlingshire
Printed and bound in Great Britain by Clays Ltd, Elcograf S.p.A.

ISBN: 978-0-241-18847-7

www.greenpenguin.co.uk

Contents

Contents

Inspector Cadaver

1. *Evening on the Local Train*

Maigret watched the world go by with large, sullen eyes, unintentionally giving himself that air of self-importance, that contrived dignity people tend to affect after hours spent sitting blankly in a train carriage. Well before the train slowed to enter the station, he saw men in voluminous overcoats spill out of every compartment, leather briefcase or suitcase in hand. Apparently oblivious to one another, they spent the rest of the journey standing in the corridor, carelessly hanging on to the brass rail across the window with one hand.

The window nearest the inspector was streaked horizontally with thick tears of rain. Gazing at that film of water, he saw the lights of a signal-box shatter into a thousand pointed rays; darkness had fallen. The next moment down below there were streets in straight lines, glistening like canals, houses, all absolutely identical, windows, doorsteps, pavements and, in that entire universe, a lone human figure, a man in a reefer jacket, hood up, on his way somewhere or other.

Maigret filled his pipe, slowly, carefully. To light it, he turned in the direction the train was travelling. Four or five passengers who were also waiting for the train to stop before hurrying off into the empty streets or making a dash for the station buffet, stood between him and the end of the corridor. Among them, he glimpsed a pale face that immediately looked away.

It was Cadaver!

The inspector's first reaction was to grumble: 'He's pretended not to see me, the idiot.'

His second was to frown. Why on earth would Inspector Cavre be going to Saint-Aubin-les-Marais?

The train slowed, came to a halt in Niort station. On the wet, cold platform, Maigret hailed a member of staff.

'Excuse me, to get to Saint-Aubin?'

'Twenty seventeen, platform three . . .'

He had half an hour to spare. After a quick trip to the public urinal at the far end of the platform, he pushed open the buffet door. He headed for one of the many unoccupied tables and sank into a chair to wait idly in the dusty light.

At the other end of the room Cadaver was sitting at an identical table without a tablecloth, still pretending not to see him.

The man's name was Cavre, Justin Cavre, not Cadaver, of course. But Inspector Cadaver was the nickname he had been given twenty years earlier and that was still what they called him at the Police Judiciaire whenever he came up in conversation.

He was a ridiculous sight off in his corner, ill at ease, twisting uncomfortably in his seat to avoid looking in Maigret's direction. It was obvious he had seen him. Lank and pasty-faced, with red eyelids, he was like one of those kids who mope around by themselves in the playground, hiding their longing to play with the other children under a sulky expression.

That was Cavre to a tee. He was intelligent. He may even, in fact, have been the most intelligent man Maigret had ever come across on the force. They were pretty much the same age, and, to tell the truth, Cavre was slightly the better educated of the two of them. Who knew, if he had persevered, he might have been promoted to detective chief inspector before Maigret.

So why had he already seemed to be carrying some sort of curse on his skinny shoulders even as a very young man? Why did he scowl at everyone as if he suspected them of wishing him ill?

'Inspector Cadaver's begun his novena . . .'

That was a phrase that used to be heard a lot in the old days at Quai des Orfèvres. On some flimsy pretext, or for no reason at all, Cavre would suddenly start giving everyone the silent, suspicious treatment. The loathing treatment, it seemed. For a week he wouldn't say a word to a soul, and his colleagues would catch him sniggering to himself, like a man who has just uncovered the darkest desires of those around him.

Not many people knew why he had suddenly quit the force. Maigret himself had only found out later and he had felt sorry for him.

Cavre was madly in love with his wife, consumed by the sort of jealous, devastating passion that you would associate with a lover rather than a husband. What could he possibly find so extraordinary about that vulgar creature with the looks of a tart or a failed starlet? The fact remained, however, that for her sake he had crossed the line in his work. Some nasty business to do with money had come to light. One evening Cavre had emerged, head bowed, shoulders hunched, from the chief's office, and a few months later they learned that he had opened a private detective agency above a stamp dealer on Rue Drouot.

People were eating dinner, each in their own little world of boredom and silence. Maigret drank a glass of beer, wiped his mouth and grabbed his suitcase. On his way out, he passed within a couple of metres of his former colleague while the latter stared fixedly at a gob of spit on the floor.

Black and wet, the local train was already on platform three. Maigret settled down in the damp chill of an old-fashioned compartment and tried unsuccessfully to close the window all the way.

There were comings and goings on the platform, those familiar noises that one absorbs unconsciously. Two or three times the door opened, a head appeared – train travellers always instinctively hunt for an empty compartment – but, at the sight of Maigret, the door quickly closed again.

As the train pulled out, Maigret went into the corridor to shut a window that was letting in a draught. In the next-door compartment, he saw Inspector Cadaver, pretending to be asleep.

For goodness' sake, it was just a meaningless coincidence. It was absurd to give it any thought. The whole business he had got himself involved in was ridiculous anyway, and Maigret wished he could just shrug it all off.

Why on earth should he care if Cavre was going to Saint-Aubin like him?

Darkness slid by outside the windows, with the occasional

gleam of light by a road: the passing headlights of a car or, more mysteriously, more appealingly, the yellowish rectangle of a window.

Bréjon, the examining magistrate – a charming, shy man with old-fashioned, punctilious manners – had told him more than once, 'My brother-in-law Naud will be waiting for you at the station. I have made sure he knows when you will be getting in.'

As he drew on his pipe, Maigret couldn't help thinking: 'What's that wretched Cadaver up to, though?'

Maigret wasn't even on an official case. Bréjon, whom he had worked with on numerous occasions, had sent him a short note asking if he would be so kind as to drop by his office for a moment.

It was January. It was raining in Paris, same as it was in Niort. There hadn't been a break in the rain or glimpse of sun for over a week. In the examining magistrate's office the lamp on the desk had a green shade. And while Monsieur Bréjon talked, incessantly wiping the lenses of his glasses as he did so, Maigret thought that there was a green lampshade in his office too, but that the magistrate's was ridged like a melon.

'. . . terribly sorry to bother you . . . especially as it is not on official business . . . Do sit down . . . Please . . . Cigar? You may know that my wife's maiden name was Lecat . . . No, no matter . . . That's not actually what I wanted to talk to you about . . . My sister, Louise Bréjon, became a Naud by marriage . . .'

It was late. People looking up from the street and seeing a light in the windows of the magistrate's office, in the

7

sombre mass of the formidable Palais de Justice, would have assumed that weighty matters were being discussed up there.

And Maigret, with his bulk and furrowed brow, gave such an impression of fierce concentration that it was unlikely anyone would have guessed what he was thinking.

Well, while listening with half an ear to the story the bearded magistrate was telling him, he was thinking about green lampshades, envying the one with ridges and dreaming of getting one like it.

'You can imagine what it's like . . . Small town, absolutely minute . . . You'll see for yourself . . . Middle of nowhere . . . Jealousy, envy, wanton malice . . . My brother-in-law couldn't be a more decent, straightforward person . . . As for my niece, she's just a child . . . If you agree, I'll put in for a week's exceptional leave on your behalf and the gratitude of my entire family, along with that which . . .'

That's how you let yourself get embroiled in a stupid escapade. What had the magistrate told him exactly? He was still a provincial at heart. And like all provincials, he loved nothing better than a long saga about local families, whose names he pronounced as if they were figures from history.

His sister, Louise Bréjon, had married Étienne Naud. As though he were speaking of someone world-renowned, the examining magistrate added, 'Sébastien Naud's son, you know . . . ?'

Sébastien Naud, it turned out, was simply a well-to-do cattle dealer from Saint-Aubin, a village lost in the depths of the Vendée marshes.

'On his mother's side, Étienne Naud is related to the finest families in that part of the world.'

Very good. And?

'They live a kilometre outside the little town, in a house practically on the railway line that runs from Niort to Fontenay-le-Comte. About two weeks ago, a young man from round there – a boy from quite a good family as a matter of fact, at least on his mother's side, who is a Pelcau – was found dead on the track. At first, everyone believed it was an accident, and I still believe that to be the case. But since then, rumours have gone round. Anonymous letters have been sent . . . To cut a long story short, my brother-in-law now finds himself in a terrible predicament – accused, virtually to his face, of killing the boy . . . He wrote me rather a vague letter about it. I in turn wrote for more information to the public prosecutor at Fontenay-le-Comte, since Saint-Aubin comes under Fontenay's jurisdiction. To my astonishment, I learned that the accusations were relatively serious and that an investigation appears inevitable . . . Which is why, my dear detective chief inspector, I ventured to call on you, as a friend, entirely . . .'

The train stopped. Maigret wiped the condensation from the window and saw a tiny building, a solitary light, a strip of platform and a lone railwayman running alongside the train, already whistling. A door slammed, and the train set off again. But not the neighbouring compartment's door; Inspector Cadaver was still on board.

They passed the odd farm, close by or off in the distance, but always down below, and whenever a light could be seen, it would invariably be reflected in a stretch of water, as if the train were skirting a lake.

'Saint-Aubin . . . !'

He gathered his things. A total of three people got off the train: an extremely old woman weighed down by a black wicker shopping basket, Cavre and Maigret. In the middle of the platform stood a very tall, very heavily built man in leather gaiters and a leather jacket, with something oddly tentative about him.

It was Naud, clearly. His brother-in-law, the examining magistrate, had told him when the inspector was coming. But which of the two men getting off the train was Maigret?

He approached the thinner of the two first. He was already raising a hand to his hat, his mouth half-open in a tentative question, when Cavre strode by disdainfully, his knowing attitude seeming to say, 'It's not me. It's the other fellow.'

The examining magistrate's brother-in-law turned on his heel.

'Detective Chief Inspector Maigret, I believe? I'm so sorry not to have recognized you immediately. Your photograph is in the newspapers such a lot . . . But in our little backwater, you understand . . .'

He had firmly relieved Maigret of his suitcase and, as the inspector searched in his pocket for his ticket, he ushered him towards the level crossing rather than the station, saying:

'There's no need . . .'

Turning to the stationmaster, he called out:

'Good evening, Pierre.'

It was still raining. A horse harnessed to a dogcart was tethered to a ring.

'Do get in. In this weather, cars can't really manage the lane.'

Where was Cavre? Maigret had seen him hurry off into the darkness. Too late he felt the urge to follow him. Anyway, wouldn't it have appeared ridiculous to leave his host stranded the minute he arrived and go dashing off after another passenger?

There was no village to be seen. Just a lamp-post, a hundred metres from the station, among a clump of tall trees by what seemed to be the start of a road.

'Spread your coat over your legs. No, you must. Even with it, your knees will get wet because the wind's against us . . . My brother-in-law wrote me a long letter about you. I am embarrassed that he should have thought to trouble a man such as yourself over such an insignificant business. You have no idea what people in the country are like.'

He touched the tip of his whip to the horse's wet hindquarters, and the wheels of the cart sank deep into the black mud of a lane that ran parallel to the railway track. On the other side, the lanterns dimly lit up some sort of canal.

A human form loomed up out of nowhere. They made out a man with his jacket over his head, who stepped aside.

'Evening, Fabien!' Étienne Naud cried out, as he had hailed the stationmaster, like a man who knows everybody, like a lord of the manor who calls everyone by his first name.

Where the hell could Cavre have got to, though? Try as he might, Maigret couldn't think about anything else.

'Is there a hotel in Saint-Aubin?' he asked.

His companion burst into good-natured laughter.

'Goodness, there's no call for a hotel! We have plenty of space at home. Your room is ready. We're having dinner an hour late because I thought you wouldn't have eaten on the way. I hope you didn't think of dining at the buffet in Niort. A terrible idea. I should warn you, though: we lay on a very simple spread.'

Maigret wasn't remotely interested in the spread they had laid on. Cavre was the only thing on his mind.

'I was wondering whether the passenger who got out when I did . . .'

'I don't know him,' Étienne Naud said hastily.

Why? That wasn't what Maigret was asking.

'I was wondering whether he'll have found somewhere to stay.'

'Of course! I don't know how my brother-in-law described our part of the world to you. Having moved to Paris, he probably thinks of Saint-Aubin as a hamlet these days. But it's almost a small town, dear sir. You haven't seen any of it because the centre is quite a distance from the station, in the other direction. There are two first-rate inns, the Lion d'Or, run by Father Taponnier, old François as everyone calls him, and, directly opposite, the Hôtel des Trois Mules . . . Look, we're almost there . . . That light you see . . . Yes . . . That's our humble abode . . .'

It was obvious just from his tone that it was going to be an imposing house, and indeed it was, vast and stocky, with four windows lit up on the ground floor and an electric light shining like a star in the middle of the façade to light the way for arrivals.

Judging from the warm, fragrant aroma that filled the air, there was a huge farmyard flanked by stables at the back of the house. A stable boy was already rushing to the horse's head, the front door was opening, a maid was coming forwards to take the guest's luggage.

'And here we are! You see, it's not far. When the house was built, unfortunately no one anticipated that one day the railway would run almost directly under our windows. Of course, one gets used to it, especially as the service is so infrequent, but . . . Do come in . . . Take off your coat . . .'

At that very second, Maigret thought, 'He has talked the whole time.'

And then he couldn't think for a moment because his mind was whirring with too many thoughts and a new atmosphere was enfolding him ever more tightly in its embrace.

The passageway was broad, with grey flagstones and walls panelled to head height in dark wood. The hall light was encased in a coloured glass lantern. A broad oak staircase with a red carpet and heavy, well-waxed banisters led upstairs. The whole house, in fact, was permeated with a rich smell of wax, of food on the simmer, and a hint of something else, something bittersweet that struck Maigret as the smell of the countryside.

What was most remarkable was the sense of peace, a peace that seemed eternal. It felt as if the furniture and all the objects in that house had been in their appointed place for generations, as if the occupants themselves in their daily round observed meticulous rituals designed to ward off the unexpected.

'Do you want to go up to your room for a moment before dinner? It's just a family home. We won't stand on ceremony.'

The master of the house pushed open a door, and two people rose simultaneously to their feet in a snug, hushed drawing room.

'May I introduce Detective Chief Inspector Maigret . . . My wife . . .'

She had the same self-effacing air as Examining Magistrate Bréjon, the same mannerliness that comes from a particular middle-class education, but for a second Maigret thought he sensed something harder, sharper in her gaze.

'I'm so sorry my brother has put you to trouble in weather like this.'

As if the rain affected his trip in any way, or was a significant part of it!

'May I introduce a family friend, inspector: Alban Groult-Cotelle, whom my brother-in-law no doubt mentioned to you . . .'

Had the examining magistrate mentioned him? Perhaps he had. Maigret had been so preoccupied with the ridged green lampshade.

'Delighted to meet you, inspector. I am a great admirer of yours . . .'

Maigret felt like replying, 'I'm not,' as he detested people of Groult-Cotelle's sort.

'Will you help us to the port, Louise?'

The bottle and glasses were laid out on a coffee table. Low, diffused lighting. Few clear-cut lines, none at all, even. Antique armchairs, most of them upholstered in tapestry. Carpets in neutral or faded colours. A log fire in the fireplace and, in front, a cat, stretching itself.

'Do sit down . . . Groult-Cotelle has dropped in for a neighbourly dinner . . .'

The latter gave an affected bow each time his name was pronounced, like a grandee who, in the company of simple folk, archly makes a point of being as formal as in high society.

'The family is so kind as to keep a regular place for me at their table, old recluse that I am . . .'

Recluse, yes, and no doubt a bachelor into the bargain. Heaven knows why you could tell, but you could. A pretentious, ineffectual character, full of quirks and eccentricities and heartily pleased to be so too.

It must have irked him not to be a count or marquis, or even have a 'de' in front of his name, but at least he had his mannered Christian name, Alban, which he loved to hear on people's lips, followed by that surname with its double barrels and hyphen.

In his forties, he was tall and slim, a combination he no doubt thought made him look aristocratic. Sprucely turned out, he nonetheless had a dusty air, which, like his dull skin and already receding hairline, struck Maigret as a sign he wasn't married. He wore elegant clothes in distinctive shades that seemed as if they had never been new, but equally, as if they would never grow old or wear out either, the sort of clothes that form an integral part of a person's character and are worn religiously like a uniform. From then on, Maigret would always see him in the same greenish, regulation country gentleman's jacket, with the same horseshoe tiepin on a white cotton piqué tie.

'Your journey wasn't too tiring, inspector?' asked Louise Bréjon, handing him a glass of port.

Ensconced in an armchair, which the lady of the house must have been worried would give way beneath him, Maigret didn't reply immediately. He was being assailed by such an array of sensations that he felt a little dazed and, for part of the evening at least, can't have made a very brilliant impression on his hosts.

There was the house first of all, this house that was the living image of the one he had so often seen in his dreams, with its reassuring walls, which made the air feel as dense as solid matter. The framed portraits reminded him of the examining magistrate's rambling account of the Nauds, Bréjons and La Noues – the Bréjons being related to the La Noues on their mother's side – and he would have happily claimed ancestry with all those solemn, slightly stiff figures.

The smells of cooking heralded an exquisite dinner, the chink of porcelain and crystal evoked a table being meticulously laid next door in the dining room. He imagined the groom rubbing down the mare in the stable, as two long rows of reddish-brown cows chewed the cud in the barn.

Everything radiated the peace of the Good Lord, order and virtue, as well as all the little mannerisms, all the charming little idiosyncrasies of simple families who lead cloistered lives.

Tall and broad-shouldered, with a ruddy complexion and prominent eyes, Étienne Naud met his gaze with complete candour, as if to say:

'You see what I'm like! . . . Straight as a die . . . Not an unkind bone in my body . . .'

The gentle giant. The good boss. The attentive father. The man who called out from his cart, 'Evening, Pierre . . . Evening, Fabien . . .'

His wife smiled timidly in the strapping fellow's shadow, as if apologizing for all the space he took up.

'If you'll excuse me for a moment, inspector . . .'

Of course. He had been expecting as much. The impeccable hostess who casts a final eye over the preparations for dinner.

Even Alban Groult-Cotelle was true to type, the more refined, better-bred, more intelligent friend. He looked as if he had stepped out of an engraving, the old friend of the family with his slightly condescending ways.

'You see,' the look in his eyes seemed to say, 'these are decent people, ideal neighbours . . . You shouldn't try to have a conversation about philosophy with them but, apart from that, you'll be very well looked after, and you'll find their Burgundy is the genuine article and their brandy deserving of the highest praise . . .'

'Dinner is served . . .'

'If you'd like to sit on my right, inspector . . .'

Weren't there any signs of anxiety, though? After all, Examining Magistrate Bréjon had clearly been concerned when he summoned Maigret to his office.

'You can understand,' he had insisted, 'I know my

brother-in-law, just as I know my sister and my niece. Besides, you will see them for yourself. Yet this vicious accusation is gaining so much ground by the day that now the public prosecutor's department is having to investigate . . . My father has been a notary for forty years in Saint-Aubin, and he took over from his father. They'll show you the family house in the middle of town . . . I can't understand how such blind hatred could have sprung up so suddenly, how it can keep on spreading, threatening to ruin innocent people's lives . . . My sister has never had a strong constitution. She's a highly strung person who has trouble sleeping and takes the least setback very hard . . .'

There wasn't a hint of any of that here. Maigret might as well just have been invited over for a good dinner followed by a hand of bridge. As a helping of roast lark was put on his plate, he was treated to a detailed explanation of how the locals literally fished the birds out of the meadows at night using nets.

Incidentally, why wasn't their daughter there?

'My niece Geneviève,' the examining magistrate had said, 'is a well-brought-up young lady, the sort you don't find any more these days except in novels.'

That wasn't the opinion of the author or authors of the anonymous letters, nor of most of the locals, who essentially accused her.

The story was still confused in Maigret's mind but it jarred so intensely with what he saw before him. According to the rumours going round, the man found dead on the railway track, Albert Retailleau, had been Geneviève

Naud's lover. It was even claimed he came to see her two or three times a week, at night, in her bedroom.

He was a lad without means, barely twenty. His father, a worker at the Saint-Aubin dairy, had died as the result of a boiler accident. His mother lived on a pension the dairy had been ordered to pay her.

'Albert Retailleau did not commit suicide,' his friends insisted. 'He enjoyed life too much. And, even if he had been drunk, as they're claiming, he wasn't stupid enough to cross the tracks when a train was coming.'

The body had been found more than five hundred metres from the Nauds', roughly halfway between their house and the train station.

Yes, but now people were alleging that the boy's cap had been found in the reeds along the canal, much closer to the Nauds' house.

And there was another, even more suspect story going round. Someone who had visited the young man's mother, Madame Retailleau, a week after the death of her son, claimed to have seen her hurriedly hiding a bundle of thousand-franc notes. As far as anyone knew, she had never had such a fortune in her life.

'It's a pity you're visiting our part of the world in the depths of winter, inspector . . . It is so beautiful round here in summer people call it the Green Venice . . . You'll have a little more pullet, won't you?'

And what about Cavre? Why had Inspector Cadaver come to Saint-Aubin?

They ate too much; they drank too much; it was too hot. In a torpor, they went back into the drawing room and sat down with their legs stretched out in front of the crackling fire.

'You must . . . I know you're particularly partial to your pipe but surely you'll have a cigar . . .'

Were they trying to pull the wool over his eyes? The idea was laughable. They were good people, nothing more and nothing less. The examining magistrate in Paris must have blown the whole affair out of proportion. And Alban Groult-Cotelle was just a po-faced idiot, one of those vaguely wealthy idlers you find everywhere in the country.

'You must be tired from your journey. When you want to go to bed . . .'

Meaning they wouldn't talk tonight. Because Groult-Cotelle was there? Or because Naud preferred not to say anything in front of his wife?

'Do you take coffee in the evening? No? No herbal tea? Will you excuse me if I go up? Our daughter hasn't been very well for two or three days and I have to go and see if she needs anything . . . Young girls are always a little fragile, you know, especially in our climate.'

The three men smoke. They talk about this and that, even local politics, because there is some story of a new mayor who is at loggerheads with all the right-thinking folk in the area and . . .

'Well, gentlemen!' Maigret finally growls with a mixture of amusement and impatience. 'If I may, I'll go to bed.'

'You'll sleep here too, Alban . . . You're not going home tonight in this weather . . .'

They go upstairs. Maigret's room is hung with yellow

wallpaper, at the far end of the passage. A real trove of childhood memories.

'You don't need anything? I was forgetting . . . Let me show you the w.c. . . .'

The men shake hands, and then Maigret undresses and gets into bed. He hears noises in the house. From very far off in his half-sleep his ears catch what sounds like the murmuring of voices, but it soon fades away, and the house becomes as quiet as it is dark.

He falls asleep, or thinks he does. He keeps seeing the dismal face of Cavre, who had to be the most miserable man on this earth, and then he dreams that the apple-cheeked maid who waited on them at dinner is bringing him his breakfast.

The door has half-opened. He is sure he has heard the door half-open. He sits up, gropes around and finally finds the pear-switch, which is hanging at the head of his bed. The bulb lights up in its frosted-glass tulip-shaped shade and he sees in front of him a girl who has put on a brown woollen coat over her night clothes.

'Sshh . . .' she whispers. 'I need to talk to you. Don't make any noise.'

And then she sits down on a chair, staring straight ahead like a sleepwalker.

2. The Girl in the Nightdress

An exhausting, yet heady night. Maigret slept without sleeping. He dreamed without dreaming, that is to say, he dreamed consciously, intentionally prolonging dreams that took their cue from real sounds.

The sound of the mare kicking its stall was real enough, for instance. But what was not, what was the result of his state of mind, was that Maigret, snug in his bed and sweating profusely, could also see the half-light of a stable, the animal's hindquarters, a little hay still in the rack and, beyond that, the rainy yard, feet splashing in black puddles, and finally, from the outside, the house in which he was staying.

It was a kind of division. Maigret was in his bed. He was intensely enjoying its warmth, the pleasurable country smell of the mattress, which became all the more pungent as he soaked it with sweat. But at the same time he was everywhere in the house. Who knows if at one point in his dream he wasn't the house itself?

He was aware of the cows stirring through the night in their barn, and at four in the morning he heard the footsteps of a stable boy crossing the yard, lifting the latch and, by the light of a storm lantern, perhaps he actually saw the lad sitting on a stool and squeezing milk into tin pails?

He must have fallen back into a deep sleep because he

started awake at the din of the lavatory flushing. He even felt afraid for a moment, the noise was so sudden and violent, but then moments later he was playing his game again, conjuring up the master of the house leaving the lavatory, his braces hanging down by his thighs, and padding back to his room. Madame Naud was sleeping, or pretending to sleep, facing the wall. Étienne Naud had only turned on the little light above the washstand. He shaved, his fingers numb from the icy water. His skin was pink, tight, shiny.

Then he sat down in an armchair to put on his boots. As he was about to leave the room, a murmur came from the blankets. What was his wife saying to him? He bent down to her, replied in an undertone, then noiselessly shut the door again and went down the stairs on tiptoe. Whereupon Maigret, who had had enough of the night's bewitchment, leaped out of bed and turned on his bedside light.

On the bedside table his watch said five thirty. He listened intently and had the impression the rain had stopped, or else had turned into a silent drizzle.

Of course he had eaten well and drunk well the night before, but he hadn't overdone it. And yet he felt as if he were waking after a night hitting the bottle. As he fished various things out of his wash bag, he stared goggle-eyed at his unmade bed, and particularly at the chair next to it.

He was sure it wasn't a dream: Geneviève Naud had been there. She had walked in without knocking. She had sat in that chair, holding herself very upright, not touching its back. In the first flush of his amazement, he had thought she was distraught. But, in fact, he was the more troubled of the two of them. He had never been in such an awkward position, lying in bed in his nightshirt, his hair mussed up, a sour taste in his mouth, as a girl settled down at his bedside to confide in him.

He had muttered something like, 'If you'd like to turn round for a moment, I'll get up and put on some clothes . . .'

'There's no need. I'll be quick. I'm pregnant with Albert Retailleau's child. If my father finds out, no one will be able to stop me killing myself . . .'

He could not even look her in the face as he was lying down. She seemed to wait for a moment to gauge the effect of her words, then got up and listened intently. As she was leaving the room, she added, 'Do whatever you want. It's completely up to you.'

He still found it hard to believe that scene was real, in which he had played the humiliating role of a prone extra. He wasn't particularly vain but he was still ashamed to have been caught in bed by a young girl, puffy and bleary-eyed from sleep. Even more demeaning was her attitude; she had barely taken any notice of him. She hadn't pleaded, as he might have expected, or thrown herself at his feet, or burst into tears.

He recalled her regular features, which looked a little like her father's. He couldn't have said if she was beautiful but he had an impression of fullness and poise that even her frenzied declaration hadn't dispelled.

'I'm pregnant with Albert Retailleau's child. If my father finds out, no one will be able to stop me killing myself . . .'

Maigret finished getting dressed, mechanically lit his first pipe of the day, opened the door and, unable to find the light switch, groped his way along the passage. He went downstairs, and at the bottom couldn't see the faintest glimmer of light but could hear the sound of a stove being raked. He headed in that direction. A streak of yellow light filtered under a door in the dining room, and, after knocking quietly, he pushed it open.

He found himself in the kitchen. Étienne Naud was sitting at the end of the table, his elbows on the light wood, eating a bowl of soup while an old cook in a blue apron dislodged a shower of glowing embers from her kitchen range.

Naud was unpleasantly surprised, Maigret could tell, but only because he had been caught eating his breakfast in the kitchen like a farm labourer.

'Already up, inspector? You see, I keep to the old country ways. Whatever time I go to bed, I'm up at five in the morning. I didn't wake you, I hope?'

What was the use of telling him the lavatory had woken him?

'I won't offer you a bowl of soup, because I suppose that . . .'

'Quite the opposite.'

'Léontine . . .'

'Yes, monsieur, I heard. Right away.'

'Did you sleep well?'

'Fairly well. I thought I heard footsteps in the passage at one point . . .'

Maigret said this to see whether Naud had caught his daughter going back to her room, but his host's surprise seemed sincere.

'When was that? In the evening? I didn't hear anything.

Although, I have to say, it does take a great deal to wake me when I'm fast asleep. Probably our friend Alban getting up to go to the w.c. . . . What do you think of that fellow? Likeable, isn't he? Much more cultivated than he lets on. You can't imagine the number of books he gets through. He knows everything, simple as that. Too bad he didn't have better luck with his wife . . .'

'He was married?'

Having marked Groult-Cotelle down as the epitome of the provincial bachelor, Maigret felt suspicious, as if they had been hiding something from him or trying to trick him.

'He not only was, he still is. He has two children, a boy and a girl. The older one must be twelve or thirteen.'

'His wife lives with him?'

'No. She lives on the Côte d'Azur. It's rather a painful story that we never refer to round here. Mind you, she was from a very good family, a Deharme . . . Yes, like the general. She's his niece . . . A slightly peculiar young woman, she couldn't seem to understand that she was living in Saint-Aubin rather than Paris . . . There were a few scandals . . . She used the pretext of a very hard winter to up sticks to Nice and has never come back. She lives down there with her children . . . Um . . . She doesn't live alone, of course . . .'

'Her husband hasn't sued for a divorce?'

'That isn't done here.'

'Which side is the fortune on?'

Étienne Naud looked at him reproachfully; he would have preferred not to have to go into details.

'She is undoubtedly very wealthy.'

The cook had sat down to grind some coffee in an old-fashioned coffee mill with a big copper lid.

'You're in luck: the rain has stopped. Still, my brother-in-law should have advised you to bring boots; he is a local, after all, and he knows these parts. We are in the depths of the marshes here. Can you believe it, to get to some of my farms, *cabanes* we call them, you have to go by boat come winter or summer! . . . Speaking of my brother-in-law, I am a little embarrassed that he dared ask someone like you . . .'

The question Maigret had been turning over in his mind since the previous evening was this: was he staying with decent sorts who had nothing to hide and were extending their warmest welcome to a guest from Paris, or was he an undesirable outsider whom Examining Magistrate Bréjon had thoughtlessly imposed on a non-plussed household who would gladly have dispensed with his services?

It occurred to him to try a little experiment.

'Not many people get out at Saint-Aubin station,' he remarked, eating his soup. 'I think yesterday there were only two of us, besides an old peasant woman wearing a bonnet.'

'That's right.'

'Is the man who alighted at the same time as me from here?'

Étienne Naud hesitated. Why? Maigret was looking at him so intently he was ashamed of his wavering.

'I'd never seen him before,' he said hurriedly. 'You may

have noticed that I couldn't decide between the two of you . . .'

Changing tactics, Maigret continued, 'I wonder why he's come here, or rather who sent for him.'

'You know him?'

'He is a private detective. I'll have to make inquiries first thing to find out what he's doing. I daresay he's staying at one of the two hotels you told me about yesterday.'

'I'll take you in a moment in the cart.'

'Thank you, but I prefer to walk, to come and go . . .'

Something had just occurred to him. Might not Naud have been thinking he could go into the village early and meet Inspector Cavre while Maigret was still asleep?

Anything was possible. The inspector found himself wondering whether the girl's visit wasn't itself part of a plan devised by the whole family.

The next moment, he was kicking himself for thinking such things.

'I hope your daughter isn't seriously ill?'

'No. If you want to know the truth, I don't think she's any more ill than I am. Despite our best efforts, she's heard whispers of what people are saying in town . . . She's proud. All young girls are. That's her real reason for hiding herself away for three days, I think . . . And, who knows, perhaps she's a little ashamed with you here?'

'My word . . .' thought Maigret, remembering the visit the young girl had paid him in the night.

'We can talk in front of Léontine,' Naud went on. 'She's known me since I was very small. She's been in the family since . . . since when, Léontine?'

'Since my first communion, sir.'

'A little more soup? No? You see, I'm in an unpleasant situation and I sometimes wonder if my brother-in-law hasn't made a mistake. You'll say he knows all this stuff better than I do because it's his job. But since he's been living in Paris, he may have forgotten the way things are around here . . .'

He seemed so happy to talk, like a man who comes right out with whatever is on his mind, it was very hard to believe he wasn't sincere. He sat there with his legs outstretched, calmly filling his pipe, while Maigret finished his breakfast. Warm and snug, the kitchen gradually filled with the smell of percolating coffee, while outside, in the darkness of the farmyard, they could hear the stable boy whistling as he groomed the horses.

'Make no mistake. Rumours do go around now and then about somebody or other. This time the accusation is a serious one, I know. But I still wonder if it wouldn't be better to treat it with contempt . . . You accepted my brother-in-law's invitation. You have done us the honour of coming. I can tell you, that will already be common knowledge. Tongues wag . . . I suppose you are going to question people? Their fancies will only get even more exaggerated. That's why I do wonder if this is the right approach . . . You're not having any more to eat? If you don't suffer too badly from the cold, I'd be delighted to show you round. I do a little tour of inspection every morning.'

Maigret was putting on his overcoat when the maid came down, her duties beginning an hour later than the old cook's. The door opened on to the cold, wet farmyard.

For an hour they went from cowshed to cowshed as milk churns were loaded on to a delivery van.

Some cows, which were leaving for a nearby market that day, were being herded together by drovers in dark smocks. At the end of the yard there was a small office with a little round stove, a desk, a stack of account-books and a row of pigeonholes. A farm worker in boots like his boss looked up as they opened the door.

'Would you excuse me for a moment?' Naud asked.

Maigret saw a solitary light on the first floor of the house. Madame Naud was getting up. Groult-Cotelle was still asleep, as was the girl. The maid was polishing in the dining room.

Meanwhile, in the darkness of the farmyard and the out-buildings, men and animals came and went as the delivery van's engine idled.

'There we are. A few instructions to give. In a moment, I'll be setting off in the car to have a look round the market. There are some fellow farmers I need to see. If I had time and I thought it would interest you, I'd explain how my business works. On my other farms, I breed ordinary herds and we also have a dairy herd. Whereas here we deal mainly in pedigree animals, which are sold abroad for the most part. I ship some as far as South America . . . Now, I am entirely at your disposal. In an hour, it will be light. If you need the car, or if you have any questions to ask me . . . I don't want to be in your way at all . . . You must treat this as your home . . .'

His face was quite open as he spoke and he showed no sign of irritation when Maigret replied:

'Well, if you have no objection, I'll go for a little explore . . .'

The lane was boggy, as though the canal, which could be seen to the left, flowed underneath it. The railway embankment ran along its right-hand side. Roughly a kilometre away an electric glare was visible. Judging by the green and red lights clustered around it, this was the station.

Turning back to the house, Maigret saw that two other windows were now lit up on the first floor, and he thought about Alban Groult-Cotelle, wondering why he had been annoyed to find out that he was married.

The sky was brightening. One of the first buildings Maigret saw, as he turned left in front of the station and went into the village, had lights on downstairs and a sign saying the Lion d'Or.

He went in and found himself in a long, low room in which everything was brown: the walls, the beams on the ceiling, the long polished tables and the backless benches. At the far end, there was an unlit kitchen range. A woman of indeterminate age, bent over a bundle of firewood burning slowly in the fireplace, was in the final stages of making coffee.

She turned for a moment to the newcomer without speaking, and Maigret sat down in the dim glow of a dust-smeared lamp.

'Give me a little glass of your local brandy, would you,' he said, shaking his overcoat, which was covered in greyish drops of dew. She didn't answer, and he thought she hadn't heard. She continued to stir her pan of unappetizing coffee and, when it was to her liking, she poured some in a cup, put it on a tray and headed for the stairs, announcing:

'I'll be right down.'

Maigret was convinced this was Cadaver's coffee, and confirmation came a few moments later when he saw the man's coat on the coat rack.

He heard footsteps overhead and the hum of voices, without being able to understand what was being said. Five minutes went by. Then another five. Every now and then Maigret rapped on the wooden tabletop with a coin to no effect.

Finally, after a quarter of an hour, the woman came back down, even unfriendlier than before.

'What did you ask me for?'

'A glass of the local brandy.'

'I don't have any.'

'You don't have any brandy?'

'I've got some cognac, but no local brandy.'

'Give me a cognac.'

She served it to him in a glass with such a thick bottom there was barely any room for the drink.

'Tell me, madame, aren't I right in saying that one of my friends stayed here last night?'

'I don't know if he's your friend.'

'Isn't he the person who's just got up?'

'I have one guest. I just took him his coffee.'

'Knowing him, I'm sure he must have bombarded you with questions. Didn't he?'

She had gone to get a cloth to wipe the tables where the previous day's customers had left wet rings.

'Didn't Albert Retailleau spend the evening before he died here?'

'What's that to you?'

'He was a good lad, I believe. I was told he'd been playing cards that evening. Is belote what people play round here?'

'Coinche is our game.'

'So he played coinche with his friends. He lived with his mother, didn't he? A fine woman, if I'm not mistaken.'

'Um . . .'

'You're saying . . . ?'

'I'm not saying anything. You're the one who's talking the whole time and I've no idea what you're driving at.'

Upstairs, Inspector Cavre was getting dressed.

'Does she live far from here?'

'Down the end of the street, at the back of a little close. The house with three stone steps . . .'

'My friend Cavre, who's staying with you, hasn't gone to see her yet, has he?'

'I'd like to know how he could have, seeing as he's only just got out of bed!'

'Is he here for a few days?'

'I haven't asked him.'

She opened the windows to push back the shutters. A milky-white sky revealed that it was already light.

'Do you think Retailleau was drunk that night?'

Suddenly aggressive, she retorted:

'No drunker than you, already on the cognac at eight in the morning!'

'What do I owe you?'

'Two francs.'

The Trois Mules inn, a slightly more modern establishment, was directly across the street, but the inspector didn't see any point going in. A blacksmith was lighting the fire in his forge. A woman on her front doorstep was throwing slops across the street. A bell tinkled shrilly, reminding Maigret of his childhood, and a kid in clogs with a loaf of bread under his arm came out of the baker's shop.

Curtains rustled as he passed. A hand wiped a steamed-up window and the deeply wrinkled face of an old woman appeared, her eyes red-rimmed like Inspector Cadaver's. The church was to the right, grey and covered with slates that were black and glistening from the rain. A woman in her fifties was coming out of it, a woman in deep mourning, very thin, very upright, holding a missal covered in black cloth in one hand.

Maigret stood idly at the corner of the square, where a road sign announced 'School' to passing motorists. He followed the woman with his eyes. At the end of the street he saw her disappear into a sort of cul-de-sac and at that moment realized it was Madame Retailleau. Thinking Cavre hadn't seen her yet, he quickened his pace.

He was right. Reaching the corner of the alley, he saw the woman climb the three steps of a little house and take a key out of her bag. Moments later, he was knocking on the glass door with a lace curtain on the inside.

'Come in.'

She had just had time to take off her coat and her mourning veil. The missal was still on the oilcloth table. A white enamel stove was already alight; meticulously clean, the top looked as if it had been scrubbed with sandpaper.

'Forgive me for bothering you, madame. Madame Retailleau, isn't it?'

He didn't feel particularly proud of himself. She didn't make a move or say a word to encourage him. She just stood there, her hands clasped on her stomach, her face almost the colour of wax, and waited.

'I have been charged with investigating the rumours concerning your son's death . . .'

'By whom?'

'Detective Chief Inspector Maigret, Police Judiciaire. I should add that at the moment my investigation is entirely unofficial.'

'What does that mean?'

'That the judicial authorities have not been formally apprised of the case.'

'What case?'

'I apologize for bringing up such painful matters but it won't have escaped you, madame, that certain rumours have been circulating about the death of your son.'

'You can't stop people talking.'

Playing for time, Maigret had turned to a photograph in an oval gilt frame that was hanging on the left of the walnut kitchen dresser.

The enlarged photograph showed a man in his thirties with cropped hair, his top lip overshadowed by a bushy moustache.

'This is your husband?'

'Yes.'

'I believe you had the misfortune to lose him in an accident when your son was still very young. From what I have been told, you were forced to take the dairy to court to get a pension.'

'Somebody's been telling you stories. There was no trial. Oscar Drouhet, the manager of the dairy, did what he had to do.'

'And then later, when your son was old enough to work, he took him on in his office. Your son was his book-keeper, I believe?'

'He did the work of an assistant manager. He would have had the title of one too if he hadn't been so young.'

'You don't have a picture of him?'

Maigret regretted asking because, as he did so, he saw a little photograph on a side table covered in red plush. He snatched it up before Madame Retailleau could object.

'How old was he when this photograph was taken?'

'Nineteen. It was last year.'

A handsome lad, healthy, vigorous, with a slightly wide face, eager lips, eyes sparkling with merriment.

Madame Retailleau stood and waited, sighing from time to time.

'He wasn't engaged?'

'No.'

'You don't know of any liaisons he may have had?'

'My son was too young to have anything to do with women. He was conscientious. All he thought about was his career.'

That wasn't the message conveyed by the young man's ardent gaze, thick, glossy hair and sturdy frame.

'What was your reaction when . . . I'm sorry . . . I'm sure you understand what I'm thinking . . . Did you believe it was an accident?'

'You can't help but believe that.'

'I mean, didn't you have any suspicions?'

'About what?'

'He had never talked to you about Mademoiselle Naud? He didn't sometimes come home late at night?'

'No.'

'Monsieur Naud hasn't paid you a visit since then?'

'We have no reason to see one another.'

'Naturally. But he might have . . . Nor Monsieur Groult-Cotelle, of course?'

Was he imagining things? It seemed to Maigret for a moment that the woman's eyes flashed with a harder light.

'No,' she said flatly.

'So you disapprove of the rumours concerning the circumstances of this tragedy . . .'

'Yes. I don't listen to them. I don't want to know about them. If you have been sent by Monsieur Naud, you can tell him what I have just told you.'

For a few seconds, Maigret remained motionless, his eyes half-shut, repeating the statement as if engraving it on his memory:

If you have been sent by Monsieur Naud, you can tell him what I have just told you.

Did she know Étienne Naud had met him at the station yesterday? Did she know Naud was indirectly responsible for bringing him here from Paris? Or did she merely suspect as much?

'Forgive me for taking the liberty of calling on you, madame, especially at such a time of day.'

'Time means nothing to me.'

'Goodbye, madame.'

She let him head for the door and shut it after himself without a word or a gesture. The inspector hadn't gone ten paces before he saw Inspector Cavre standing on the kerb as if on guard duty.

Was Cavre waiting for Maigret to come out before calling on Albert's mother himself? Maigret wanted to know for sure. The conversation he'd just had had put him in a bad mood, and he could think of worse things than playing a trick on his former colleague.

Relighting his pipe, which he had put out with his thumb before going into Madame Retailleau's, he crossed the street, took up position on the kerb directly opposite Cavre and stood there as if resolved not to budge.

The town was coming alive. Children could be seen flocking to the school gates on the little church square. Most came from far afield, wrapped up tight in scarves and wearing thick red or blue woollen socks and clogs.

'Well, my old Cadaver, your turn! Off you go!' Maigret seemed to say, his eyes sparkling mischievously.

But Cavre didn't move, except to look off in the other direction as if he were above jokes of any sort.

Had Madame Retailleau hired him to come to Saint-Aubin? It was possible. She was a curious woman, difficult to pin down. There was something of the farmer's wife about her; she had their almost congenital distrust. But she also reminded him of the provincial *haute bourgeoisie*.

He suspected her icy manner concealed an unshakeable pride and he had been impressed by her restraint. The entire time he had been in her house, she hadn't taken a step or made a gesture. She had been frozen, like one of those animals that supposedly play dead in the face of danger, with only the barest movement of her lips as she uttered the occasional syllable.

'Well, Cadaver, you poor thing? Make your mind up. Do something.'

Cadaver was stamping his feet to keep warm, but didn't seem inclined to do anything as long as Maigret was spying on him.

The situation was ridiculous. It was childish to persist, and yet Maigret persisted. All to no avail, what's more. At eight thirty, a little red-faced man emerged from his house, headed to the town hall and opened its front door with his key. Moments later, Cavre entered the premises.

That was exactly what Maigret had intended to do first: go and question the local authorities. His former colleague had beaten him to it. Now there was nothing for him to do but wait his turn.

3. A Man You Would Keep at Arm's Length

Subsequently, that day became a taboo subject for Maigret. He never spoke about it again, especially not about that morning, and he doubtless did his utmost not to think about it either.

What he found most disconcerting was the way he had simply ceased to be Maigret. After all, what did he represent in Saint-Aubin? Nothing. For goodness' sake, Justin Cavre had simply marched into the town hall ahead of him, and Maigret had been left standing sheepishly in the street, surrounded by those houses, which, under a sky like a blister about to burst, looked like fat, poisonous toadstools.

People were watching him, he knew. Eyes were fixed on him behind every curtain. Of course, the opinion of some old women or the butcher's wife didn't matter; people could think whatever they wanted of him. They could even, as some kids had done on their way to school, burst out laughing when he walked past.

But he was conscious of not being the usual Maigret. It may be an exaggeration to say he did not recognize himself, but that was partly it.

What would happen, for instance, if he went into the whitewashed lobby of the town hall and knocked on the grey door with the words 'Secretary's Office' written across it in black letters? He would be asked to wait his turn, as if he were applying for a birth certificate or welfare. And, meanwhile, in that stuffy little office, Cadaver could carry on questioning the secretary at his leisure.

Maigret wasn't there in an official capacity. He couldn't invoke the Police Judiciaire. As for his name, who knew if anyone had heard of it in this village surrounded by slimy bogs and pools of stagnant water?

He would soon find out for himself. Kicking his heels, he waited for Cavre to reappear and then had one of the most outlandish ideas of his career. He was within a whisker of latching on to his former colleague, dogging his every step, and saying point-blank:

'Listen, Cavre, it's not worth us trying to outsmart one another. You're not here just for the hell of it. Somebody sent for you. Tell me who it is and what they've got you doing . . .'

How simple a proper, official investigation seemed to him at that moment! If he had been on a case somewhere under his jurisdiction, he would merely have had to go into the post office, pick up the telephone and say:

'Detective Chief Inspector Maigret. Put me through to the Police Judiciaire immediately . . . Hello! . . . Is that you, Janvier? Jump in a car . . . Get over here . . . When you see Cadaver come out . . . Of course, Justin Cavre . . . Fine . . . Follow him, yes, don't take your eyes off him . . .'

Who knows? He might also have put a tail on Étienne Naud, whom he had just seen go by at the wheel of his car, heading to Fontenay.

It was so easy being Maigret. You had a whole apparatus of the most sophisticated kind at your disposal. And you only had to casually drop your own name for people to be so dazzled they would bend over backwards to be agreeable to you.

Whereas here he was such an unknown that, despite all the articles about him, all the photographs of him in the papers, Étienne Naud had marched up to Justin Cavre at the station.

Naud had made him welcome because of the examining magistrate brother-in-law who had sent him from Paris, but hadn't they all seemed to be wondering why he was there? The subtext to Naud's reception was more or less:

'My brother-in-law Bréjon is a charming fellow who clearly wishes us well, but he's been gone from Saint-Aubin too long and he's got some strange ideas into his head about this business. It was good of him to think of sending you here, and it was good of you to have come. We are going to look after you to the best of our abilities. So, eat, drink, come on the tour of the property with me and, whatever you do, don't feel under any obligation to stay a moment longer in this damp, charmless little town. Nor to get involved in this wholly insignificant business that is just between us.'

Whom was he working for, when it came down to it? Étienne Naud. Well, Étienne Naud would obviously rather he didn't conduct a serious investigation.

As for the incident in the night, that beat everything. Geneviève coming into his room to tell him, essentially, 'I was Albert Retailleau's mistress. I am pregnant with his child. But if you say a word I'll kill myself.'

Well, if she really was Albert's mistress, the accusations

against Naud acquired a terrible plausibility. Had she thought of that? Had she knowingly accused her father?

And what about the victim's mother? She hadn't said anything or asserted anything or denied anything; she had simply intimated, with every fibre of her being:

'What business is any of this of yours?'

To everyone, even the old ladies hiding behind their quivering curtains, even the kids just now who had turned to stare after they had passed him, he was the intruder, the undesirable. No, worse, he was totally untrustworthy, a stranger who had just turned up from who knew where to do who knew what.

All of which meant that, particularly in those streets, with his hands thrust in the pockets of his big overcoat, he felt like one of those sordid characters tormented by a secret perversion who skulk around Porte Saint-Martin and the like, their shoulders hunched, their faces twisted, hugging the walls whenever they see someone from the vice squad.

Was this Cavre's influence? Maigret felt like fetching his suitcase from the Nauds', catching the first train and telling Examining Magistrate Bréjon, 'They don't want me there. Let your brother-in-law manage by himself . . .'

Nonetheless, he went into the town hall as Cavre walked away. The former inspector had a leather briefcase under his arm, which no doubt conferred some special status on him in the eyes of the townsfolk, elevating him to a member of the legal profession.

The little town clerk, who smelled bad, did not stand up as he entered his office.

'May I help you?'

'Detective Chief Inspector Maigret of the Police Judiciaire. I'm in Saint-Aubin in an unofficial capacity and I'd like to ask you for some information.'

The other hesitated irritably before pointing Maigret to a rush-seated chair.

'Did the private detective who just left say who he was working for?'

The secretary did not understand, or pretended not to understand, the question. The same, pretty much, applied to all the inspector's other questions.

'You knew Albert Retailleau. Tell me what you thought of him.'

'He was a good lad . . . Yes, that's a fair description: a good lad. You couldn't lay any faults at his door.'

'Did he chase after women?'

'He was a young man, wasn't he? You never really know what young people get up to. But you definitely wouldn't say he chased after women.'

'Were he and Mademoiselle Naud lovers?'

'People have claimed as much. There were rumours. But it was just talk, as rumours only ever are.'

'Who found the body?'

'Ferchaud, the stationmaster. He telephoned the town hall, and the deputy mayor immediately called the gendarmerie at Benet, because we don't have a squad in Saint-Aubin.'

'What did the doctor who examined the body say?'

'What did he say? That he was dead. There wasn't much of a body to examine, strictly speaking . . . The train had run over it . . .'

'But it was still identified as Albert Retailleau?'

'What? Of course. It was definitely Retailleau, no doubt about that.'

'When had the last train gone by?'

'Seven minutes past five.'

'People didn't find it strange that Retailleau was found on the railway track at five o'clock in the morning in the middle of winter?'

The secretary's response was priceless:

'It was dry. Frosty.'

'Even so, rumours have gone round . . .'

'Rumours, yes. You can't stop rumours.'

'Your personal opinion is that it was an accident?'

'It is very hard to form an opinion.'

Maigret tried mentioning Madame Retailleau:

'A wonderful woman. That's all there is to say about her.'

He raised Naud for discussion:

'Such an agreeable person. His father, who was a general councillor, was also a real gentleman.'

Finally, he asked about the girl:

'A pretty young lady . . .'

'Well behaved?'

'Of course she is well behaved. And her mother is one of the finest people in this town.'

The little man said all of this without conviction, politely at best, as he foraged in his nose and examined the results with interest.

'Monsieur Groult-Cotelle?'

'An extremely decent fellow too. No airs and graces.'

'Is he a very close friend of the Nauds?'

'They often see one another, yes. They move in the same circles, don't they?'

'What day was Retailleau's cap found not far from the Nauds' house?'

'What day? Well . . . But was that all that was found?'

'I was told that someone called Désiré, who collects milk for the dairy, had found the cap in the reeds by the canal.'

'People have said as much . . .'

'It's not true?'

'It is hard to know whether it is true. Désiré is drunk half the time.'

'And when he's drunk?'

'One minute he says yes, the next he says no.'

'But a cap! It's something visible, tangible. People have seen it.'

'Ah.'

'It must be somewhere now . . .'

'Perhaps . . . I don't know. You see, we're not the police, we only concern ourselves with our own business . . .'

You couldn't make yourself plainer than this grubby, gormless little fellow, who was delighted to have shut the Parisian up.

Maigret was outside in minutes, back to square one, or rather now certain that no one was going help him discover the truth.

And if no one wanted the truth, what had he come here for? Wouldn't it be better to go back to Paris and tell Bréjon, 'There it is . . . Your brother doesn't want there to be an investigation into the affair. No one in the

46

town does. I've come back. They gave me a first-rate dinner . . .'

A gilt plaque indicated the notary's residence, which must have been the one belonging to Bréjon's father and his sister, now Madame Naud. It was a large grey-stone building and, against the damp grey of the sky, it looked as eternal and inscrutable as the rest of the town.

He passed the Lion d'Or. The landlady was in conversation with someone, and he sensed they were talking about him, standing by the window to get a better view.

A cyclist approached. Maigret recognized him but didn't have time to turn around. It was Alban Groult-Cotelle, who was cycling back from the Nauds'. He jumped off his bike.

'I'm so glad to run into you. My house is just around the corner. Will you do me the pleasure of coming and having a drink? You must . . . My house is a very modest affair, but I do have a few bottles of vintage port.'

Maigret followed his lead. He didn't have high hopes but anything was better than dragging himself around the streets of this hostile town.

The house was huge. It looked attractive from a distance, solid and stocky, like a bourgeois fortress with its black railings and high slate roof.

Inside, everything smelled of meanness and neglect. The sulky maid looked really unkempt and yet, from their eye contact, Maigret gathered that Groult-Cotelle was sleeping with her.

'Excuse the mess. I'm a bachelor, living on my own. Apart from books, I don't really have any interests, so . . .'

So the wallpaper was damp and peeling off the walls, the curtains were grey with dust, and Maigret had to test three or four chairs before finding one that stood securely on all four feet. Probably to save wood, only one room in the house was heated, on the ground floor, and this served as drawing room, dining room and library. There was even a divan on which he suspected his host slept more often than not.

'Please, do sit down. It really is a shame you're not visiting in summer, when our town is rather more presentable . . . What do you think of my friends, the Nauds? What a lovely family they are! I know them well. You won't find a better man than Naud. Not a very deep thinker perhaps. Perhaps a shade pleased with himself. But so guileless, so sincere. He is very rich, you know?'

'And Geneviève Naud?'

'A charming girl . . . Not overwhelmingly so . . . Yes, charming's the word . . .'

'I suppose I'll get the chance to see her. She'll only be temporarily indisposed, won't she?'

'I daresay . . . I daresay . . . Young girls, eh? Your health . . .'

'You knew Retailleau?'

'By sight. His mother is apparently a very fine woman . . . If you were staying a while, I'd show you round, because you really can find some interesting people here and there, in the villages . . . My uncle, the general, used to say that the countryside, especially where we are in the Vendée . . .'

Useless! If Maigret had let him, Groult-Cotelle would

have recited the histories of every local family from scratch.

'I have to be on my way . . .'

'Your investigation, that's true. Is it getting anywhere? Do you have hopes? In my opinion, you need to get your hands on the person who is behind all these false rumours . . .'

'Do you have any ideas?'

'Me? Hardly! Don't go supposing I've got an inkling about this business, will you now. I'll probably see you this evening because Étienne has invited me to dinner, and, unless I'm too busy . . .'

Busy doing what, for goodness' sake? Words seemed to mean something different in this part of the world.

'Have you heard anything about the cap?'

'What cap? Ah, yes. I'd lost the thread. I vaguely remember hearing something . . . Is it true, though? Has it really been found? That's the key, isn't it?'

It wasn't the key, no. The girl's confession, for instance, was just as significant as the discovery of the cap. But could one use that confession?

Five minutes later, Maigret was ringing the doctor's doorbell. A petite maid told him at first that the practice didn't open for an hour, but when he insisted, she showed him into a garage, where a strapping, red-faced fellow was repairing a motorcycle.

The usual refrain:

'Detective Chief Inspector Maigret . . . Police Judiciaire . . . In an entirely unofficial capacity . . .'

'Let's go into my consulting room and I'll wash my hands.'

Maigret waited near the articulated table covered with an oilcloth that was used for examining patients.

'So you're the famous Detective Chief Inspector Maigret. I've heard a great deal about you. I have a friend thirty-five kilometres away who follows all the news avidly. If he knew you were in Saint-Aubin, he'd drop everything . . . You were in charge of the Landru case, weren't you?'

He had lighted on one of the few cases in which Maigret hadn't played a part.

'To what do we owe the honour of your presence in Saint-Aubin? Because it certainly is an honour . . . You'll have a glass of something, I trust . . . One of my little ones happens to be sick, and we've put him in the sitting room because it's warmer. That's why I'm seeing you here . . . A little glass, eh?'

He was true to his word. Maigret got his little glass and not a drop more.

'Retailleau? A nice lad. I think he was a good son. At any rate, his mother, who is one of my patients, never complained about him. She is quite something, that woman. She deserved a very different life. She was from a good family, you know. We were extremely surprised when she married Joseph Retailleau, who was just a worker at the dairy . . .

'Étienne Naud? He's a character. We go shooting together. He's a first-rate shot . . . Groult-Cotelle? No, you wouldn't say he was a marksman, but that's because he's very short-sighted . . .

'So you already know everyone . . . Have you met Tine too? You haven't made Tine's acquaintance yet? Notice the respect with which I utter that name, like everyone in Saint-Aubin. Tine is Madame Naud's mother. Madame Bréjon, if you'd rather. She has a son who's an examining magistrate in Paris. Of course, you must know him . . . She was born a La Noue herself, one of the great Vendée families. She doesn't want to be a burden on her daughter and son-in-law, and she lives alone, near the church . . . At eighty-two, she is still hale and hearty, and she is one of my most incorrigible patients . . .

'Are you staying a few days in Saint-Aubin?

'What? The cap? Oh, yes! No, I haven't heard anything about it myself . . . Well, I did hear some vague rumours . . .

'You understand, all this is a bit after the fact. If I had known at the time I would have performed a post-mortem. But put yourself in my position. I'm told the poor boy has been run over by a train. I establish that he has indeed been run over by a train and so, naturally, I write my report to that effect.'

Maigret glowered. He could have sworn that they were all in collusion, that, whether surly or breezy like the doctor, they were all batting him back and forth like a ball while exchanging knowing winks.

The sky has almost cleared. There are reflections in all the puddles and the mud is glistening in places.

Once again the inspector sets off along the main street – whatever it's called; he hasn't seen yet, but he's pretty sure it will be Rue de la République – and thinks he might as well go into the Trois Mules opposite the Lion d'Or, where he had been made so unwelcome that morning.

The parlour is lighter, with whitewashed walls hung with framed colour prints and a photograph of a president of the Republic from thirty or forty years ago. Beyond it there is another bleak, empty room with paper streamers and a stage, the Sunday dance hall.

Four men are sitting at a table around a bottle of rosé. When the inspector comes in, one of them coughs pointedly, as if announcing to the others, 'Here he is . . .'

Maigret sits on one of the benches at the opposite end of the room. And this time, he feels that something has changed. The men have fallen silent. Before he came in they were certainly not sitting there drinking with their elbows on the table, staring at each other speechlessly.

They act out a dumb show, their elbows moving closer, their shoulders brushing, until finally the oldest, who has a ploughman's whip at his side, directs a long stream of spit at the floor, which causes laughter.

Is that spit for Maigret's benefit?

'What can I get you?' a woman comes to ask him. Still young, she has a grubby-faced baby on her hip.

'Some rosé.'

'A half bottle?'

'If you like . . .'

He takes small, sharp draws on his pipe. This isn't the latent or muted hostility he has encountered thus far; he is being taunted now, provoked almost.

'What do you want me to say, son, it takes all trades,' says the ploughman after a long silence, without anyone having asked him anything.

The others burst out laughing, as if these simple words

mean a great deal to them. Only one doesn't laugh, a youngster, a kid of eighteen or nineteen with light-grey eyes and a face pitted with smallpox scars.

Leaning on one elbow, he looks Maigret in the eye as if he wants to make him feel the full weight of his hatred or contempt.

'You've got to have some pride, though!' another growls.

'When there's money involved, pride never gets much of a look-in . . .'

This may not really mean anything, but Maigret has understood. He has finally found the opposition party, to use a political term.

Who knows? No doubt the Trois Mules is the source of all the rumours that have been going around. And these people are attacking him because they think he's being paid by Étienne Naud to hush up the truth.

'Tell me, gentlemen . . .'

He has got to his feet. He has started walking towards them and, although he does not suffer from shyness, he feels his ears burning.

Absolute silence greets him. Only the young man carries on looking him full in the face. The others turn away, a little embarrassed.

'As you're locals, perhaps you could answer some questions for me and let justice take its course . . .'

They are suspicious. Of course the notion appeals to them, but they are not about to give in just like that. The old man grumbles, looking at his spit spangling the floor:

'Whose justice? Naud's?'

As if he hasn't heard, the inspector carries on, while the landlady, baby on hip, comes and stands in the kitchen door.

'For that to happen, there are two things in particular that I need to find. First, a friend of Retailleau: a real friend, and someone, if possible, who was with him on his last night . . .'

A nod from the three men towards the youngest tells Maigret that the latter fits this description.

'Then I have to get my hands on the cap. You know the one I mean.'

'On you go, Louis!' growls the ploughman, rolling a cigarette.

But the young man is not convinced yet.

'Who sent you?'

It's the first time Maigret has ever been compelled to account for himself to a young country lad. But there's no alternative. He has to win this fellow over.

'Detective Chief Inspector Maigret of the Police Judiciaire.'

Who knows? By some chance, the kid may have heard of him. Unfortunately his name doesn't prompt even a flicker of recognition.

'Why did you stay at Naud's?'

'Because he'd been told I was coming and he picked me up at the station. As I wasn't familiar with the town . . .'

'There are hotels.'

'I didn't know that.'

'Who's the guy who's staying across the road?'

'A private detective.'

'Who's he working for?'

'I don't know.'

'Why hasn't there been an investigation yet? Albert died three weeks ago.'

'Good work, son! On you go!' the three men seem to be encouraging the teenager as he fights against shyness, his whole body rigid with the effort.

'No one lodged a complaint.'

'So, you can kill someone and, as long as there's no complaint . . .'

'The doctor declared it an accident.'

'Was he there when it happened?'

'As soon as I've gathered sufficient evidence, the investigation will become official.'

'What do you call evidence?'

'If it could be proved, for instance, that the cap was discovered between the Nauds' house and the place where the body was found.'

'Should take him round to Désiré,' says the fattest of the men, in carpenter's overalls. 'Same again, Mélie. Bring another glass.'

That in itself is a victory for Maigret.

'What time did Retailleau leave the café that night?'

'Eleven thirty, maybe . . .'

'Were there many people there?'

'Four. We'd been playing coinche.'

'You all left together?'

'The other two headed off to the left. I went some of the way with Albert.'

'In which direction?'

'To the Nauds'.'

'Did he confide in you?'

'No.'

The young man has grown melancholy. He shakes his head regretfully, visibly trying to be scrupulously honest.

'He didn't tell you why he was going to the Nauds'?'

'No. He was furious.'

'Who with?'

'With her.'

'Mademoiselle Naud, you mean? He'd talked to you about her before?'

'Yes.'

'What had he told you?'

'This and that . . . Nothing in particular . . . He went there almost every night.'

'He bragged about it?'

'No,' the lad says with a reproachful look. 'He was in love and it showed. He couldn't hide it.'

'And on the last day, he was furious?'

'Yes. All evening, playing cards, his mind was elsewhere, and he kept looking at the clock. On the path, when he left me . . .'

'Where?'

'Five hundred metres from the Nauds' place.'

'So, where he was found dead?'

'Roughly . . . I had taken him halfway . . .'

'And you're sure he went on?'

'Yes. He told me, with tears in his eyes, holding both my hands, "It's over, Louis, my old friend . . ."'

'What was over?'

'Between him and Geneviève. That's what I understood. He meant he was going there for the last time.'

'But did he go there?'

'There was a moon that night. It was freezing. I saw him again when he was no more than a hundred metres from the house.'

'And the cap?'

Young Louis gets up, looks at the others with a resolute air.

'Come on . . .'

'Do you trust him, Louis?' asks one of the older men. 'Watch out, my son.'

But Louis is of an age when you don't hold back. He looks Maigret in the eye as if to say, 'You're the lowest of the low if you let me down!'

'Follow me. It's just round the corner.'

'Your glass. Here's to you, inspector . . . You can believe everything the kid tells you, that's the main thing. He's as honest as the day is long, that boy.'

'Your good health, gentlemen.'

He toasts them, not that he has any choice. The big glasses clink, and then he follows Louis out, forgetting to pay for his wine.

As he steps outside he sees Cadaver on the other side of the road, heading back to the Lion d'Or, his briefcase under his arm. Is Maigret mistaken? He has the impression that a sardonic smile passes over the face of his former colleague, which he only sees in profile.

'Come here . . . This way . . .'

The two of them make their way along a network of

back alleys connecting the town's three or four streets that Maigret hadn't suspected existed.

In one of those rows of little houses fronted by tiny gardens with picket fences, Louis pushes open a gate with a bell hanging on it and calls out, 'It's me!'

He goes into a kitchen where four or five children are sitting round a table having lunch.

'What is it, Louis?' asks his mother, giving Maigret an embarrassed look.

'Wait for me here . . . Just a moment, sir . . .'

He rushes up the stairs which lead straight off the kitchen and goes into a bedroom, where he can be heard opening a chest of drawers. Then he starts pacing up and down, knocking over a chair, while his mother, who isn't sure whether she should make Maigret welcome, closes the door behind him anyway.

Pale and agitated, Louis storms back down.

'It's been stolen!' he announces, glowering.

Then turning to his mother, he says harshly:

'Someone's been here . . . Who? Who was here this morning?'

'Now, Louis . . .'

'Who? Tell me who! Who stole the cap?'

'I don't even know what cap you're talking about . . .'

'Someone went up to my room . . .'

He is so overexcited he looks as if he's going to hit his mother.

'Will you calm down! Can't you hear how you're speaking to me?'

'Were you in the whole time?'

'I went to the butcher and the baker.'

'And the kids?'

'I left them next door, as usual. The two youngest, who aren't at school yet.'

'I'm sorry, inspector. I just can't make this out. The cap was still in my drawer this morning. I'm sure of it. I saw it . . .'

'But what cap do you mean? Will you answer me? Bless me, anyone would think you've gone mad! You'd be better off sitting down and having something to eat . . . As for this gentleman you've just left standing here . . .'

But Louis, with a sharp, suspicious look at his mother, ushers Maigret outside.

'Come on. There's more I need to tell you . . . I swear on my father's grave that the cap . . .'

4. The Cap Theft

The impatient kid walked quickly, his neck taut, his body bent forwards, dragging along in his wake the heavy-set Maigret, who was uncomfortable with the whole set-up. What a sight the two of them must make, the garrulous, persuasive younger one leading him on like one of those Montmartre touts you see escorting an intimidated gent almost against his will to some dubious entertainment or other.

As they were already turning the corner of the lane, Louis' mother, standing on her doorstep, called out, 'Aren't you coming to eat, Louis?'

It was doubtful whether he even heard. He was obsessed. He had promised this gentleman from Paris something and now an unforeseen event meant that he couldn't keep his word. He'd be taken for a charlatan! His cause would be compromised!

'I want you to hear it from Désiré himself. The cap was there, in my room. I wonder if my mother was telling the truth . . .'

Maigret wondered the same thing and thought of Inspector Cavre as he did so. He didn't imagine a mother of six would present much of a challenge for him.

'What time is it?'

'Ten past midday . . .'

'Désiré will still be at the dairy. Let's go this way. It's quicker.'

He kept to the back alleys as before, and they passed mean little houses that took Maigret by surprise. Somewhere a mud-spattered sow threw itself at their shins.

'One night at the Lion d'Or – wait, the night of the funeral, in fact – old Désiré came in, threw a cap on the table and asked in patois whose it was. I recognized it immediately, because I'd been with Albert when he bought it in Niort, and we'd talked about the colour.'

'What's your trade?' asked Maigret.

'Joiner. The biggest one of that lot in the Trois Mules just now is my boss. The evening I'm telling you about Désiré was drunk. There were at least six people in the café. I asked him where he'd found the hat. He collects milk from the little farms in the marshes, you see, and, as you can't get to them by lorry, he does his rounds by boat . . .

'"I found it in the reeds," he told me, "just by the dead poplar . . ."

'As I said, at least six people were there who heard him say that. Everyone round here knows that the dead poplar is between the Nauds' house and the place where Albert's body was found . . .

'This way . . . We're going to the dairy, you can see the chimney on the left . . .'

They had left the village. Dark hedges surrounded small gardens. A little further on, the dairy came into view, a collection of low buildings painted white and a tall chimney rising sheer into the sky.

'I don't know why I thought of sticking the cap in my pocket. I already had the feeling too many people wanted this business hushed up.

'"That's young Retailleau's cap," someone said.

'And Désiré, even though he was drunk as a lord, frowned. He knew very well that he shouldn't have found it where he did.

'"Are you sure, Désiré, that it was near the dead poplar?"

'"Why wouldn't I be sure?"

'Well, inspector, the next day he wouldn't admit it. When you asked him where it was, he'd answer, "Over there . . . I don't know exactly, do I? Why don't you give it a rest about that cap?"'

Some flat-bottomed boats filled with milk churns were moored next to the dairy.

'Hey, Philippe. Has old Désiré gone home?'

'He can't have gone home seeing as he never set foot out of doors. He must have had a skinful last night because he hasn't done his round this morning.'

An idea occurred to Maigret.

'Do you think the manager will be here now?' he asked his companion.

'He should be in his office. The little door on the side.'

'Wait here a moment.'

Oscar Drouhet, the manager of the dairy, was in fact making a telephone call as Maigret opened the door. He introduced himself. The man had the serious, steady air of all rural artisans turned small manufacturers. Taking small puffs on his pipe, he studied the inspector and let him speak as he sized him up.

'Albert Retailleau's father used to be on your staff, didn't he? From what I've been told he was the victim of a work accident . . .'

'A boiler ring blew.'

'I understand you pay the widow a fairly high pension?'

The man was quick, realizing immediately that it was a loaded question.

'What do you mean?'

'Did the widow take you to court or did you set it up of your own accord?'

'Don't go looking for any mystery in all this. It was my fault the accident happened. Retailleau had been telling me for two months, more or less, that the boiler needed a complete overhaul, if not replacing. As it was the height of the season, I kept putting it off.'

'Your workers were insured?'

'Inadequately.'

'Sorry. May I ask whether it was you who thought the sum inadequate or . . . ?'

They had already understood each other so well that Maigret left his sentence unfinished.

'The widow put in a claim, as she was entitled to,' admitted Oscar Drouhet.

'I am certain,' continued the inspector with a hint of a smile, 'that she didn't seek you out merely to ask you to study the question of compensation. She sent lawyers . . .'

'Is that so strange? A woman isn't an expert in these matters, is she? I recognized the validity of her claim and, in addition to the pension paid by the insurance, I set up one that I pay personally. I also paid for the son's education and I took him on here as soon as he was old enough to work. I got a lot out of it too, because he was an honest, hardworking, clever lad, who could run the dairy while I was away . . .'

'Thank you . . . Or rather, one more thing: since Albert's death, you haven't received a visit from his mother?'

Drouhet managed not to smile, but a glint passed through his brown eyes.

'No,' he said, 'she hasn't come *yet*.'

So Maigret hadn't been mistaken about Madame Retailleau. She was a woman who knew how to defend herself, even go on the attack if necessary, and who never lost sight of her interests.

'Apparently Désiré, your milk collector, didn't come to work this morning?'

'That happens with him. Days when he's drunker than usual . . .'

Maigret rejoined the pockmarked teenager, who was terrified he wasn't being taken seriously any more.

'What did he tell you? He's a good guy, but he's part of the other lot, really . . .'

'What other lot?'

'Monsieur Naud, the doctor, the mayor . . . He couldn't turn you against me, though . . .'

'No, of course not . . .'

'We've got to find old Désiré. Let's go to his place, if you don't mind. It's not far.'

They set off again, both forgetting that it was lunchtime. At the entrance to the village, they went round to the back of a house. Louis knocked on a glass door, then pushed it open and shouted into the semi-darkness:

'Désiré! Hey! Désiré . . .'

Only a cat came to rub itself against his leg, while Maigret peered into what looked like an animal's den. There was a bed without sheets or pillow, on which one would have had to sleep fully dressed, a small cracked cast-iron stove and a jumble of clothes, empty litre bottles and gnawed bones.

'He must be drinking somewhere. Come on.'

Still the same fear of not being taken seriously.

'He worked on Étienne Naud's farm once, you see. Even though he was sacked, he stayed on good terms with them. He's the sort of person who likes staying on good terms with everybody. That's why, the day after the one I told you about, he put on a big act when he was asked about the cap: "What cap? . . . Oh yes, that rag I picked up somewhere, I'm not sure where any more. I don't even know where it's got to . . ."'

'Well, sir, I can tell you for a fact that there were blood-stains on the cap, as I wrote to the prosecutor . . .'

'You wrote the anonymous letters?'

'I wrote three, at least. If there were any others, they weren't by me. I wrote about the cap, then about Albert going with Geneviève Naud . . . Wait, maybe Désiré is here . . .'

It was a grocer's but, through the windows, Maigret saw that there were bottles on the end of the counter and two tables, at the back of the room, where people could have a drink. The kid emerged empty-handed.

'He came by early this morning. He must have visited all the chapels . . .'

Until then, Maigret had known of only two cafés in Saint-Aubin, the Lion d'Or and the Trois Mules. He now added at least a dozen more to that total in less than half an hour – not cafés as such but drinking dens that would have been invisible to the average passer-by. The saddler ran one next to his workshop. There was another in the blacksmith's. And old Désiré had been seen at all, or almost all, of them.

'How was he?'

'He was fine.'

It was obvious what that meant.

'He was in a hurry when he left because he had something to do at the post office . . .'

'The post office is closed,' Louis said. 'I know the postmistress. You just have to knock on the window. She'll open up for you.'

'Especially because I have a telephone call to make,' said Maigret.

And indeed, as soon as the kid knocked on the glass, the window opened a crack.

'Is that you, Louis? What do you want?'

'The gentleman from Paris needs to make a telephone call.'

'I'll open up right away.'

Maigret asked to be put through to the Nauds'.

'Hello! Who's calling?'

He didn't recognize the voice, a man's.

'Hello! What's that? Ah, sorry . . . Alban, yes . . . I didn't understand . . . Maigret here . . . Would you tell Madame Naud that I won't be coming back for lunch . . . Apologize to her for me . . . No, nothing important . . . I don't know when I'll be back yet . . .'

Coming out of the booth, he saw from his companion's face that he had some interesting information to relay.

'How much do I owe you, mademoiselle? Thank you. I'm sorry to have disturbed you.'

In the street, Louis announced in a state of high agitation:

'I told you something was up. Old Désiré came on the stroke of eleven. Do you know what he did at the post office? He sent a postal order for five hundred francs to his son in Morocco . . . His son is a bad lot, who up and left one day just like that. When he was here, the old man and him quarrelled and fought non-stop. Désiré has always been blind drunk as long as we can remember. His son writes to him now and again, always complaining and asking for money. But all the money goes on drink, see? The old man never has a sou. Sometimes, at the start of the month, he sends a postal order for ten or twenty francs . . . I wonder . . . Wait . . . If you still have some time, we'll go and look in at his sister-in-law's.'

The inspector was becoming familiar with the streets and houses he had passed repeatedly since that morning. He recognized the faces as he went by, the names painted over the shops. Rather than brightening up, the sky was getting dark again, and the air was growing thick with moisture. The fog hadn't rolled in yet but it was on its way.

'His sister-in-law does knitting. She's an old girl who was the last priest's maid. Look, it's here . . .'

He climbed the three steps of a porch, knocked and opened a door painted blue.

'Désiré isn't here, is he?'

He immediately waved Maigret over.

'Hi, Désiré . . . I'm sorry, Mademoiselle Jeanne. There's a gentleman from Paris who'd like to have a quick word with your brother-in-law.'

The table was laid in a small, very clean room, near a mahogany bed covered with a huge red eiderdown. There was a sprig of box tucked into a crucifix, a virgin under a glass dome on the chest of drawers and two cutlets on a plate with an illustration and a motto.

Désiré made a move to get up, before realizing he was in danger of falling off his chair. Maintaining a dignified stillness instead, he muttered, his tongue so thick that he could hardly articulate the syllables:

'How can I be of service to you?'

He had manners, clearly. That was something he was keen to stress himself.

'I may have been drinking . . . Yes, I may have had a little drink, but the thing about me, sir, is that I am polite. Everyone will tell you that Désiré is polite to everyone he meets . . .'

'Listen, Désiré, the gentleman needs to know where you found the cap . . . You know, Albert's cap . . .'

That was enough. Clouding over with a look of utter stupor, the drunkard's face became blank, his watery eyes even more opaque.

'. . . don't know what you mean . . .'

'Stop fooling around, Désiré. Anyway, I've got that cap

myself. You remember that evening when you threw it on the table at François', saying you'd found it near the dead poplar . . .'

The old ham didn't simply deny it. He contorted his face into a series of grimaces, throwing himself into his role with far more gusto than was necessary.

'Understand what he's going on about, do you, sir? Why would I have thrown a cap on the table, eh? Never worn a cap in my life . . . Jeanne! Where's my hat? Show the gentleman my hat . . . Those kids, they've got no respect for age.'

'Désiré . . .'

'What do you mean, "Désiré?"? Désiré may be drunk, but he is polite and he requests that you call him Monsieur Désiré . . . Understand, you brat, you bastard?'

'Have you heard from your son?' Maigret broke in abruptly.

'Well, what about my son? What's he done, my son? My son's a soldier, for a start! He's a brave man, my son!'

'That's what I meant. I'm sure he'll be glad to get his postal order.'

'Don't I have the right to send my son a postal order now? Hey, Jeanne! Do you hear that? Perhaps I'm not allowed to come and have a bite with my sister-in-law either?'

He may have been afraid initially but now he was enjoying himself. He was overacting with such a will that, when Maigret left, he staggered after him to the door and would have followed him on to the street if Jeanne hadn't stopped him.

'Désiré has manners . . . Understand, you little brat? And you there, my Parisian friend, if anyone tells you Désiré's son isn't a brave man . . .'

Doors opened. Maigret chose to walk away.

With tears in his eyes, Louis said through gritted teeth, 'I swear to you, inspector . . .'

'Yes, son, I believe you.'

'It was that man who stayed at the Lion d'Or, wasn't it?'

'Yes, I'm sure it was. I'd like to have proof, though. Do you know anyone who was at the Lion d'Or last night?'

'I bet the Liboureau kid was there. He goes there every night.'

'Well then, while I wait for you at the Trois Mules, go and ask him if he saw old Désiré in there and if he got into conversation with the visitor from Paris . . . Wait . . . I suppose you can eat at the Trois Mules? We'll have a bite together . . . Be quick about it.'

There was no tablecloth. The cutlery was iron. There was only beetroot salad, rabbit and a piece of cheese washed down with a wretched bottle of white. But when he came back, Pockmarks was too shy to sit at the inspector's table.

'Well?'

'Désiré went to the Lion d'Or yesterday.'

'He talked to Cadaver?'

'To what?'

'Take no notice. It's a nickname we gave him. Did he talk to him?'

'That wasn't what happened. The character you call Ca . . . It makes me feel strange saying it . . .'

'His name is Justin Cavre.'

'From what Liboureau told me, Monsieur Cavre spent most of the evening watching people playing cards without saying anything. Désiré was off in a corner, drinking on his own. He left about ten o'clock and a few minutes later Liboureau noticed the Parisian wasn't there any more. But he didn't know if he'd gone out or upstairs.'

'He went out.'

'What are you going to do?'

Proud to be the inspector's accomplice, Louis was seething with impatience to act.

'Who was it who saw a large sum of money at Madame Retailleau's?'

'The postman, Josaphat. He's another drinker. We call him Josaphat because when his wife died he got even more cock-eyed than usual and wouldn't stop crying and saying: "Goodbye, Céline. We'll meet again in the valley of Josaphat, we will. Count on me . . ."'

'What would you rather for dessert?' asked the landlady, who clearly spent her days with one or other of her children on her arm, doing her work one-handed. 'I've got biscuits and apples.'

'You choose,' said Maigret.

And the other, blushing:

'I don't mind . . . Biscuits . . . This is what happened. Maybe ten or twelve days after Albert's funeral, the postman had a pick-up at Madame Retailleau's. She was doing the housework. She looked in her purse but she was fifty francs short. So she went over to the soup tureen on the dresser. You must have noticed it. A tureen with blue flowers. She stood in front of it to block Josaphat's view, but that evening he swore he'd seen a wad of thousand-franc notes, at least ten, maybe more . . . Well, everyone knows Madame Retailleau has never been able to get her hands on that much money . . . Albert spent everything he earned . . .'

'On what?'

'He cared about his looks. It's not a crime, is it? He loved being well dressed and he had his suits made in Niort. He was always ready to stand a round. He used to tell his mother that she had her pension, after all . . .'

'They used to argue?'

'Sometimes. Albert was independent, you know? His mother would have liked to treat him like a kid. If he'd listened to her, he wouldn't have gone out at night and he'd have never set foot in the café. My mother is the opposite. All she asks is that I'm out of the house as much as possible.'

'Where can we find Josaphat?'

'He should be at home now, or else on his way back from his first round. In half an hour, he will be at the station to pick up the bags for the second post.'

'Please will you bring us two digestifs, madame?'

Through the curtains, Maigret looked at the windows opposite and imagined Cadaver having his lunch and watching him back. Reality soon intervened, however, as a car noisily announced its presence and stopped outside the Lion d'Or. Cavre got out, his briefcase under his arm, and bent down to the driver to haggle over the price.

'Whose car is that?'

'The mechanic at the garage's. We passed it just now. He runs a taxi service occasionally when someone's going to hospital or needs something urgently from the shops . . .'

The car turned around and, judging by the sound, only drove a short distance before stopping again.

'You see. He's gone back to his place.'

'Do you get on well with him?'

'He's a friend of my boss.'

'Go and ask him where he went this morning with his fare.'

Less than five minutes later, Pockmarks came running back.

'He went to Fontenay-le-Comte. That's dead on twenty-two kilometres from here.'

'You didn't ask him where in particular?'

'He was told to stop at the Café du Commerce, Rue de la République. The Parisian went in, then came out with someone and told the driver to wait.'

'You didn't find out who his companion was?'

'The mechanic doesn't know him . . . They were gone for half an hour. Then your Cavre asked to be driven back. He only gave him a five franc tip . . .'

Hadn't Étienne Naud gone to Fontenay-le-Comte too?

'Let's go and see Josaphat.'

He had already left home. They caught up with him at the station, where he was waiting for the train. When he saw Pockmarks and Maigret appear at the far end of the platform, he seemed annoyed and rushed into the station-master's office as if he were busy.

They waited for him all the same.

'Josaphat!' called Louis.

'What do you want? I don't have time for you.'

'There's someone who'd like to have a quick word with you.'

'Who's that? I'm working, and when I'm working . . .'

Maigret had a struggle ushering him to an empty spot between the lamp store and the urinals.

'A simple question . . .'

He was obviously on his guard. He pretended to hear the train, to be poised to make a dash for the mail van. At the same time he couldn't help darting filthy looks at Louis, who had put him in this situation.

Maigret already knew he wouldn't find out anything. His colleague Cavre had clearly beaten him to it.

'Hurry up, I can hear the train . . .'

'You picked something up a fortnight or so ago from Madame Retailleau.'

'I'm not allowed to talk about work matters.'

'But you did that evening.'

'In front of me!' the kid broke in. 'Avrard was there, Lhériteau, little Croman . . .'

The postman shifted from foot to foot, a stupid and insolent look on his face.

'What gives you the right to interrogate me?'

'We can ask you a question, can't we? You're not the Pope, are you?'

'What if I asked this man who's been skulking around town since morning for his papers? Eh?'

Maigret had already turned around, realizing it was

pointless to insist. Louis, however, shocked by such dis-
honesty, lost his temper.

'You'd have the nerve to say that you didn't talk about
some thousand-franc notes that were in the tureen?'

'Why not? What are you going to do about it?'

'You talked about them. I'll get the others to tell it to
your face too. You said the notes were pinned together . . .'

The postman walked away, shrugging. This time the
train really was pulling in and he took up position where
the mail van always stopped.

'The shyster!' Louis growled between his teeth. 'You
heard him, didn't you? Honestly, though, you can believe
me . . . Why would I lie? I knew this would happen.'

'Why?'

'Because it's always the same when they're involved . . .'

'Who?'

'All of them. I don't know how to explain it. They stick
up for each other. They're rich. They're all relatives or
friends of chiefs of police, generals, judges. I don't know
if that makes any sense. Anyway, people are scared. Sometimes, of course, they'll talk late at night when they've had
a bit to drink, but the next day they regret it. What are you
going to do? You're not going back to Paris?'

'Of course not, son. Why?'

'I don't know. That other man looks . . .'

The kid bit his tongue just in time. He was obviously
going to say something along the lines of, 'He looks
tougher than you!'

And it was true. In the fog that was starting to come
down like an artificial dusk, Maigret thought he saw

Cavre's sallow face, his fleshless lips stretched in a sardonic smile.

'Isn't your boss going to say anything about you not being at work yet?'

'Oh no! He's not like that at all. If he could help us prove poor Albert was murdered, he would, I tell you . . .'

Maigret jumped as a voice behind him asked, 'The Lion d'Or hotel, please?'

The railwayman on duty by the ticket barrier pointed to the street that started a hundred or so metres away.

'Straight ahead. You'll see, on your left.'

A plump, immaculately dressed little fellow went out, dragging a suitcase that seemed as big as him and looking around for a non-existent porter. The inspector scrutinized him from head to toe, but without success. He didn't know him.

5. Three Women in a Drawing Room

'If you need me, I'll be at the Trois Mules all evening,' Pockmarks said, before he rushed off into the fog and was swallowed up.

It was five o'clock. With the fog, darkness had fallen. Maigret had to walk the length of Saint-Aubin's high street before reaching the station and the lane leading to Étienne Naud's house. Louis had offered to show him the way, but you had to draw the line somewhere, and Maigret had had enough of virtually being dragged along by the hand by the hectic, feverish young man.

As he was leaving him, Louis had said reproachfully, almost sentimentally, 'Those people,' he meant the Nauds, of course, 'will fawn all over you and you'll end up believing everything they tell you.'

Hands in pockets, overcoat collar turned up, Maigret made his way cautiously towards the first light he could see, which resembled a lighthouse in the fog. Although it seemed a long way off, the shimmering halo was so bright it was easy to think he was heading for a major landmark. Moments later he almost walked straight into the chilly window of the Vendée Cooperative, which he must have already passed twenty times that day. A narrow green shop, repainted fairly recently, its window display consisted of the sort of glass and earthenware objects that businesses give away as complimentary gifts.

Further on, in the pitch dark, his coat snagged on a hard object, and he groped around mystified for a long while, before finally realizing that he had wound up among the carts that stood, their shafts in the air, outside the cartwright's.

The bells rang out suddenly just above his head. He was passing the church. The post office was to the right, with its dolls' house wicket gate; facing it was the doctor's house.

The Lion d'Or café on one side, the Trois Mules on the other. It was incredible to think that wherever a light showed there were people living in a tiny circle of warmth. They were like incrustations on the frozen wastes of the universe.

Saint-Aubin wasn't a big place. He could already see the lights of the dairy like a factory ablaze in the night. A train's engine in the station spat fire.

This was the miniature world in which Albert Retailleau had lived. His mother had spent her whole life here. Apart from holidays at Les Sables-d'Olonne, someone like Geneviève Naud had virtually never left this little town.

When the train had slowed down a little just before Niort station, Maigret had seen empty, rainswept streets, rows of gaslights, houses like blind people, and he had thought, 'There are people who spend their whole lives in one of those streets.'

Testing the ground with his foot, he was now making his way along the canal towards the next lighthouse in sight, the light shining at the Nauds'. Looking out from trains, on cold nights, or in driving rain, he had seen other equally remote houses. A yellow rectangle of light is the only sign that they exist. Your imagination races. You speculate.

And now here he was, entering the realm of one of those lights. He climbed the steps and, as he looked for the bell, he saw the door wasn't shut. He went into the hall, purposely dragging his feet to announce his presence, but that wasn't enough to interrupt the monotonous monologue that he could hear in the drawing room to his left. He took off his wet coat and hat, wiped his feet on the doormat and knocked.

'Come in. Geneviève, open the door . . .'

He had already opened it. In the drawing room, where only one of the lamps had been turned on, he found Madame Naud sewing by the fireplace, a very old woman sitting opposite her, and a young girl who was coming towards him.

'I'm sorry to disturb you . . .'

The girl looked at him anxiously, not knowing whether he was going to betray her. He merely bowed to her.

'My daughter, inspector. She has been so keen to meet you since she's started feeling better. Let me introduce you to my mother . . .'

So this was Clementine Bréjon, née La Noue, whom everyone familiarly called Tine. Small and brisk, with a grimacing face reminiscent of a bust of Voltaire, she stood up and asked in an odd falsetto:

'Well, inspector, have you had your fill of turning our poor Saint-Aubin on its head? Ten times – no, more! – I saw you march up and down, and this afternoon I noticed that you had gained a recruit . . . Do you know who's been acting as the inspector's mahout, Louise?'

Was 'mahout' chosen expressly to emphasize the disparity between the thin Louis and the elephantine Maigret?

Louise Naud, who had inherited very little of her mother's briskness, and whose face was much longer and paler, remained bent over her sewing, nodding and giving the occasional wan smile to show she was paying attention.

'Fillou's son. It was bound to happen. The boy must have lain in wait for him. I daresay he's been regaling you with some fine stories, inspector?'

'Not at all, madame. He simply took me to one person or other whom I was keen to see and who would otherwise have been difficult to find. The townspeople on the whole are not particularly talkative . . .'

The girl had sat down and was staring at Maigret as if hypnotized by him. Madame Naud occasionally looked up from her handiwork and cast a furtive glance at her daughter.

The drawing room was just as it had been the day before, all the objects were in their appointed place, a heavy peace prevailed, and yet the grandmother's presence was the only normal thing about it.

'I am an old woman, inspector, so I can remember another affair like this one, only much more serious, which almost had Saint-Aubin up in arms. In those days, there was a clog factory that employed fifty men and women. It was when strikes were breaking out constantly all over France and the workers would process through the streets over the least little thing . . .'

Madame Naud had raised her head to listen. Maigret saw an expression of barely concealed anxiety on her thin face, which looked exactly like Examining Magistrate Bréjon's.

'One of the workers at the clog factory was called Fillou. He wasn't a bad fellow but he liked a drink and when he had been drinking he fancied himself as a public speaker. What did really happen? Well, one day he went in to see his boss with some complaint or other. Not long afterwards, the door opened and Fillou came flying out, as if he had been shot by a catapult, staggered backwards for several metres and then fell into the canal.'

'Was he the father of young Pockmarks?' asked Maigret.

'His father, yes. He's dead now. At the time, you had to be for or against Fillou or the boss. One side claimed that Fillou was drunk and acting like a lunatic, and that the clog-maker had been forced to remove him bodily, the other that it was the boss who was entirely to blame. He was supposed to have said hateful things about the workers, such as: "I can't help it if they keep producing more urchins when they're drunk on a Saturday night . . . "'

'Fillou died, did you say?'

'Two years ago. Of stomach cancer.'

'Were many people on his side when this was happening?'

'Not the majority, but his supporters were the most rabid, and every morning people would find threats written on their doors in chalk.'

'You mean to say, madame, that the two cases are alike?'

'I don't mean to say anything at all, inspector. You know how old people like to ramble on. In small towns, there is always a Fillou affair or a Retailleau affair, otherwise life would be too monotonous. There is always a little group that is beside itself with rage . . .'

'What was the upshot of the Fillou affair?'

'Nothing. Silence, of course . . .'

Ah yes, silence, Maigret thought. The little group of radicals can agitate as much as it likes, the silence is always stronger. He had come up against that silence all day.

There was something else he had been feeling since he had sat down in the drawing room which unsurprisingly made him uneasy.

Having wandered sullenly and doggedly about the streets in Pockmarks' wake from dawn to dusk, he had absorbed some of the lad's outraged determination.

'She's one of them . . .', Louis would have said.

And being *one of them*, in Louis' mind, meant signing up to the conspiracy of silence; joining the group that didn't want any fuss, that was bent on living as if everything was for the best in the best of all worlds.

Deep down, Maigret sided with the little group of rebels. He had drunk their health at the Trois Mules. He had disowned the Nauds by saying he wasn't working for them. And when the kid doubted him, he had all but given him his word.

But Louis still hadn't been mistaken when, as he left the inspector, he had looked at him suspiciously, dimly sensing what would happen when his companion was the enemy's guest again. That was why he had tried to take him to the door. He had wanted to fire him up, to steel him against any weakness.

'If you need me, I'll be at the Trois Mules all evening . . .'

He would wait in vain. In the bourgeois hush of that drawing room, Maigret almost felt ashamed to have run around the streets in the company of a kid and been sent packing by all the people he had got it into his head to question.

On the wall there was a portrait that Maigret had not noticed the night before, a portrait of Examining Magistrate Bréjon, who seemed to be staring at the inspector as if to say, 'Don't forget the task I entrusted you with . . .'

He watched Louise Naud's fingers as she sewed and was mesmerized by their jitteriness. Her face was almost serene, but her fingers revealed a fear bordering on panic.

'What do you think of our doctor?' asked the chatty old lady. 'A character, isn't he? The mistake all of you make in Paris is to think that there aren't any interesting people in the countryside. If you stayed here just a couple of months . . . I say, Louise, isn't your husband coming home?'

'He telephoned just now to say he would be late because he had to go to La Roche-sur-Yon. He asked me to apologize to you, inspector . . .'

'I owe you an apology, too, for not having come back for lunch.'

'Geneviève! You should give the inspector a drink.'

'Well now, children, it's time I got going.'

'Stay and have dinner with us, Maman. Étienne will drive you home when he gets back.'

'Nay, my girl. I don't need anyone to drive me home.'

Her daughter helped her tie the ribbons of a little black cabriolet hat perched jauntily on her head, and slip galoshes over her shoes.

'You don't want me to have the horses put to?'

'There will be plenty of time to put the horses to on the day of my funeral. Goodbye, inspector. If you pass under my windows again, come and say a quick hello. Good night, Louise. Good night, Viève . . .'

And then suddenly, as the door closed behind her, there was a gaping void. Maigret understood why they had tried to stop old Tine leaving. With her gone, the silence pressed down on their shoulders, weighty and nerve-racking, and something like fear could be felt crawling through the room. Louise Naud's fingers ran faster and faster over her handiwork as the girl searched for an excuse to leave but didn't dare get up.

Wasn't it shocking to think that while Albert Retailleau was dead, found one morning torn to pieces on the railway track, his child was alive in the room at that moment, a living being that would be born in a few months?

When Maigret turned to the girl, she didn't look away. Quite the opposite. She sat up and looked straight at him, as if to say, 'No, you didn't dream it. I came into your room last night and I wasn't sleepwalking. What I told you then is the truth. You can see I'm not ashamed of it. I'm not mad. Albert was my lover and I am pregnant with his child . . .'

So, the son of Madame Retailleau, who had stood up so doughtily for her rights when her husband died, Pockmarks' young, passionate friend, used to slip undetected into this house at night. Geneviève would be waiting for him in her room at the end of the passage in the right wing.

'Will you excuse me, mesdames? If you have no objection, I'd like to go for a quick walk round the yards and outbuildings.'

'Do you mind if I come with you?'

'You'll catch cold, Geneviève.'

'I won't, Maman. I'll wrap up.'

She brought a stable lantern, already lit, from the kitchen. In the hall Maigret helped her put on a cloak.

'What do you want to see?' she asked in a whisper.

'Let's go to the yard.'

'We can go this way. No need to go all through the house . . . Watch out for the steps . . .'

There were lights on in the stables, and the doors were open, but the fog was so thick it was impossible to make anything out.

'Your room's the one right above us, isn't it?'

'Yes. I see what you mean. He didn't use the front door, obviously . . . Come here. You see that ladder. We always left it here. He only had to move it a few metres.'

'Where is your parents' room?'

'Three windows along.'

'And the other two windows?'

'One is the guest room, where Alban slept that night. The other is a room that hasn't been used since my little sister died in it. Only Maman has a key.'

She felt the cold but was trying not to show it, in case it seemed as if she wanted to end their conversation.

'Your parents never suspected anything?'

'No.'

'Had your liaison been going on for long?'

She didn't have to rack her brains.

'Three and a half months.'

'Retailleau knew the consequences of your love?'

'Yes.'

'What was he planning to do?'

'To confess everything to my parents and marry me.'

'Why was he furious that last night?'

Maigret stared at her, trying as best he could to make out her features in the fog. The ensuing silence revealed her astonishment.

'I asked you . . .'

'I heard.'

'Well?'

'I don't understand. Why do you say he was furious?'

Her hands were shaking like her mother's, as was the lantern.

'Nothing special had happened that evening?'

'Nothing, no.'

'Albert left by the window as usual?'

'Yes. There was a moon. I saw him walk off towards the bottom of the yard, where he could climb over the little wall and take the lane . . .'

'What time was it?'

'Twelve thirty, maybe . . .'

'Were his visits usually so brief?'

'What do you mean?'

She was playing for time. Through a window not far from them they could see the old cook moving about.

'He got here around midnight. I assume he wouldn't usually have been in such a hurry to leave . . . Did you have an argument?'

'Why would we have had an argument?'

'I don't know. I'm asking you.'

'No.'

'When was he supposed to talk to your parents?'

'Soon. We were waiting for the right moment . . .'

'Think carefully . . . Are you sure you didn't see any lights on in the house that night? Didn't you hear any noise? Was anyone hiding in the yard?'

'I didn't see anything. I swear, inspector, I don't know anything. You may not believe me, but it's the truth . . . I'll never, you hear, never tell my father what I told you last night . . . I'll go away . . . I don't know what I'll do . . .'

'Why did you tell me?'

'I don't know . . . I was afraid . . . I imagined you would find out, that you'd tell my parents everything . . .'

'Let's go in, shall we? You're shivering.'

'You won't tell?'

He didn't know what to say. He didn't want to commit himself with a promise, so he muttered:

'Trust me.'

Had he become *one of them*, as Pockmarks would have said? Oh, he understood that lad's expression all too well now. Albert Retailleau had died and been buried. And now there were plenty of people in Saint-Aubin, the majority in fact, who thought that, since the young man couldn't be brought back to life, the wisest course of action would be never to mention him again.

Being one of them was being part of that clan. Retailleau's mother, who hadn't seemed to understand why an investigation was being launched, was one herself.

And those who weren't initially had been won over one by one. Désiré had changed his mind about finding the cap. What cap? He had enough money to drink his fill and send his bad lot of a son a postal order for five hundred francs.

Josaphat, the postman, had no recollection of any thousand-franc notes in the soup tureen.

And Étienne Naud was at a loss as to why his brother-in-law would send a man like Maigret. The inspector seemed to have got it into his head that he had to discover the truth.

But what truth exactly? And if it ever was discovered, what, and who, would it be for?

That only left the little gang in the Trois Mules. A joiner, a ploughman and a kid called Louis Fillou, whose father was a hothead anyway, obsessively telling their stories.

'You're not hungry, inspector?' asked Madame Naud as Maigret came into the drawing room. 'Where's my daughter?'

'I've just left her in the hall. I imagine she's gone up to her room for a second.'

There followed a genuinely desperate quarter of an hour. The two of them were alone in the old-fashioned, overheated drawing room. From time to time a log collapsed in the fireplace with a shower of sparks. A pink lampshade on the only light that was switched on softened all the colours. Not a sound was to be heard, apart from the occasional, familiar sound of something in the kitchen, the stove being stoked, a pot being moved, an earthenware plate being set on the table.

Louise Naud would have liked to talk. It was obvious

from her manner. She was possessed by a demon that urged her to say . . .

To say what? She was in pain. Sometimes she would open her mouth, full of resolve, and Maigret was afraid of what was coming . . .

But then she didn't say anything. A nervous spasm would clutch her chest, her shoulders would quiver for a second, and then she would carry on sewing with small stitches, crushed by that weight of stillness and silence that trapped them both.

Did she know that her daughter and Retailleau . . .

'Do you mind if I smoke, madame?'

She started, perhaps afraid he had been going to say something else, and stammered:

'Please . . . You must think of this as your home . . .'

Then she sat up straight, listening intently.

'Oh goodness . . .'

Oh goodness what? She was waiting for her husband to come back, for anyone to appear who would put an end to the torment of this tête-à-tête.

Maigret felt remorse. What was stopping him from getting to his feet and saying, 'I think your brother made a mistake asking me to come here. There's nothing I can do. This affair is none of my concern and, if you don't mind, I'll take the first train to Paris. I am very grateful for all your hospitality.'

He saw Pockmarks' pale face again, his fiery eyes, his sardonic mouth.

Most of all, though, he saw Cavre's silhouette, with his briefcase under his arm; Cavre, who finally, after so many years, happened by pure chance to have been granted the opportunity to triumph over his hated former boss.

Because Cavre loathed him. He loathed everybody, naturally, but he loathed Maigret in particular. Maigret, whom he considered as his alter ego, a successful version of himself.

He had outmanoeuvred him at every turn, it seemed, since the moment they had stepped off the train, and Naud had almost got them mixed up.

Where was that clock he could hear ticking?

Maigret looked round the room for it. He was gripped by a deep sense of unease. He thought to himself, 'Another five minutes and this poor woman is going to throw a fit. She'll blurt out the truth. She can't take it any more. She's at the end of her tether . . .'

He only needed to ask her a direct question. Or not even that. He could just go and stand in front of her and look searchingly into her eyes. Would she be able to resist?

Instead of which, he not only kept silent but even, to put her at ease, discreetly reached for a periodical lying on a side table. It was a women's magazine devoted to embroidery patterns.

As in a dentist's waiting room, where you read things you wouldn't think of reading anywhere else, Maigret slowly turned the pages, attentively studying the pink and blue illustrations, without the invisible bond between him and his hostess slackening for a moment.

It was the maid who saved them. She was a young, rough-and-ready country girl, whose black dress and white apron brought out her strong, irregular features.

'Oh, sorry! . . . I didn't know there was anyone . . .'

'What is it, Marthe?'

'I was wondering if I should lay the table or if I should wait for monsieur . . .'

'Lay the table!'

'Is Monsieur Alban coming to dinner?'

'I don't know. Lay his place anyway . . .'

What a relief to utter everyday words, to talk about simple, reassuring things! She clutched at the subject of Alban.

'He came for lunch today. That's right, when you rang, he picked up the telephone. He leads such a lonely life! We've come to think of him as one of the family . . .'

Now that an opportunity to escape had finally presented itself, she seized it.

'Will you excuse me for a moment? A mistress of the house, you know . . . Always something to keep an eye on in the kitchen . . . I'll ask the maid to tell my daughter to come and keep you company . . .'

'Don't trouble yourself, please . . .'

'In any case . . .' She listened intently. 'Yes . . . There's my husband . . .'

A car stopped at the base of the steps, its engine still running. Voices could be heard. Maigret wondered if his host had brought someone, but he was merely giving some instructions to a servant who had rushed out to the car.

Naud pushed open the door of the drawing room before he had taken off his leather coat. Astonished to find them in a tête-à-tête, he gave them an anxious look.

'Oh! You're . . .'

'I was just telling the inspector, Étienne, that I had to leave him for a moment to go and check in the kitchen . . .'

'My apologies, inspector. I am on the General Council's Agricultural Board and I had forgotten we had an important meeting today . . .'

He sneezed and poured himself a glass of port, trying as he did to work out what might have happened in his absence.

'Well, has your day been a success? I was told on the telephone that you didn't have time to come back for lunch.'

He was afraid of a tête-à-tête too. He looked at the armchairs in the drawing room as if reproaching them for being unoccupied.

'Alban hasn't put in an appearance?' he asked with feigned bonhomie, turning towards the dining-room door, which was still open.

His wife's voice answered from the kitchen:

'He had lunch with us. He didn't say if he'd be coming back.'

'Geneviève?'

'She went up to her room.'

He didn't dare take a seat or settle down anywhere. Maigret understood, and almost shared, his anguish. In order to feel strong, or simply not start trembling, they had to be together, shoulder to shoulder; the family circle had to be unbroken.

Only then could they recreate the usual atmosphere of the house for the inspector's benefit. They supported each other, making trivial remarks that blended into one another to form a sort of reassuring purr.

'A glass of port?'

'I've just had one.'

'You'll have another, I trust . . . So . . . Tell me what you've been doing . . . Or rather . . . I mean, I don't want to pry . . .'

'The cap has disappeared,' Maigret declared, staring at the carpet.

'Ah, yes, really? The famous cap that was supposed to prove the crime . . . So where was it? Believe it or not, I've always wondered if it really existed . . .'

'Someone called Louis Fillou claims it was in his chest of drawers.'

'It was in Pockmarks' house? And you say it was stolen this morning? Don't you find that a little odd?'

He burst out laughing as he stood there, so tall and strong, so sturdy and ruddy-cheeked. The owner of the house, the head of the family, just back from debating regional governmental affairs in La Roche-sur-Yon. He was Étienne Naud, Squire Naud, as the locals would have said, the son of Sébastien, a man who was himself known and respected throughout the département.

But there was fear in his laughter as he reached for a glass of port, his eyes searching in vain for the usual support of his family. He would have liked to have his whole entourage around him, his wife, his daughter and Alban, who, on that day of all days, had seen fit to stay away.

'A cigar . . . No? . . . Are you sure . . . ?'

He paced round and round the drawing room, as if taking a seat meant falling into a trap, delivering himself bound hand and foot to this appalling detective chief inspector whom his idiotic brother-in-law had sent to ruin his life.

6. Groult-Cotelle's Alibi

An incident occurred, which, although trivial in itself, nonetheless set Maigret thinking. It was before dinner. Étienne Naud still hadn't been able to bring himself to sit down, as if he were afraid he would be even more at the inspector's mercy once he was at rest. Madame Naud and her maid could be heard in the dining room, engaged in a discussion about poorly cleaned silverware. Geneviève had just come downstairs.

Maigret caught the look her father gave her as she came into the drawing room. It was slightly anxious. Of course Naud hadn't seen his daughter since the day before, when she had been ill. And it was also only natural that Geneviève should reassure him with a smile.

Just at that moment, the telephone rang, and Naud went out into the hall to answer it. He left the door open.

'What?' he exclaimed in astonishment. 'For goodness' sake, of course he's here . . . What's that? Yes, hurry up, we're expecting you . . .'

When he returned to the drawing room, he shrugged again.

'I wonder what's got into our friend Alban. He's had a regular place at our table for years. Then this evening he calls me to ask me if you're here and, when I say you are, he asks my permission to come for dinner and adds that he needs to speak to you . . .'

Maigret happened to be looking at the daughter rather than the father. He was taken aback by the fierce expression on her face.

'That's what he did earlier, pretty much,' she said testily. 'He came for lunch and, when he saw the inspector wasn't here, he seemed put out. I thought he was going to go. He stammered, "What a pity. I had something to show him . . ." Then he left immediately after bolting his dessert. You saw him in town, I suppose, inspector?'

It was so subtle that it was impossible to put into words. A nuance in the girl's voice. Or not really in her voice, even. What is it, for instance, that makes an experienced man suddenly realize a young girl has become a woman?

Maigret's intuition was of a similar sort. Geneviève's irritability struck him as more than just an ordinary bad mood, and he resolved to keep a closer eye on Mademoiselle Naud.

Madame Naud came in, apologizing, and her daughter took the opportunity to repeat. 'Alban just rang to inform us that he's having dinner with us. But only after he had asked if the inspector had come back. We're not the attraction . . .'

'He'll be here in a moment,' said her father, finally sitting down now the family was reunited. 'It'll only take him a few minutes on his bike.'

Maigret remained sitting quietly in his seat, looking somewhat dejected. His large eyes were expressionless, as they always were whenever he found himself in an awkward situation. He observed each of them in turn, giving a ghost of a smile when anyone spoke to him, and thought, 'How they must curse their blundering idiot of a brother-in-law and me! They all know what happened, including their friend Alban. That's why they start shaking the minute they're apart. When they're together they can reassure each other, present a united front . . .'

What had really happened? Had Étienne Naud found young Retailleau in his daughter's bedroom? Had an argument broken out between them? Had they had a fight? Had Naud simply shot him down like a rabbit?

What they must have gone through that night. The mother beside herself with panic, the servants, who would have been scared if they had heard something . . .

There was a tap at the front door. Geneviève made a move as if to open it but then remained in her chair, and Naud, a little surprised, as if this wasn't the usual way of things, went out into the hall. They heard him chatting about the fog, and then the two men came back in together.

As a matter of fact, this was the first time Maigret had seen the young girl and Alban in the same room. She held out her hand to him rather stiffly. He bowed, kissed the back of her fingers, then hurriedly turned to Maigret, anxious to tell him or show him something.

'Would you believe it, inspector, this morning after you left I happened to lay my hands on this . . .'

And he held out a little strip of paper that, judging by two little prick marks in the top corner, had been pinned to other pieces of paper like it.

'What is it?' Naud inquired casually, as a look of distrust crossed the girl's face.

'You've always made fun of my mania for keeping every last scrap of paper. I could find the paltriest little laundry bill from three, or even eight, years ago . . .'

The piece of paper Maigret was turning over in his thick fingers was a receipt from the Hotel de l'Europe in La Roche-sur-Yon. *Room: 30 francs. Breakfast: 6 francs. Service . . .*

Date: 7 January.

'Of course,' Alban said with an apologetic air, 'it's not remotely important. But I remembered that the police like alibis. Look at the date. As chance would have it I was in La Roche, as you can see, on the night when the person of whom you know met his death . . .'

Naud and his wife responded like society people confronted by a display of bad manners. Madame Naud looked at Alban in astonishment, as if she wouldn't have expected such a thing from him, then, with a sigh, lowered her eyes to the logs in the fire. Her husband merely frowned. He was slightly slower on the uptake, or perhaps was trying to find a hidden meaning in his friend's behaviour.

As for Geneviève, she had gone white with rage. She was clearly shocked. Her eyes glittered. Maigret stared fixedly at her, so fascinated was he by her reactions of the past few minutes.

Tall and thin, with a receding hairline, Alban remained standing somewhat sheepishly in the middle of the drawing room.

'At least you're not waiting to be accused of anything

before you mount your defence,' Naud declared eventually, having had time to weigh his words.

'What on earth do you mean, Étienne? I get the feeling you've all misinterpreted this. Just now, while I was filing some papers, by pure chance I happened to come across this hotel bill. I thought it would be interesting to show it to the inspector, given that it is the very date when . . .'

Madame Naud broke in, a rare occurrence for her.

'You've already told us,' she said. 'I think we can sit down . . .'

The discomfort lingers. The meal may be as meticulous and brilliant a success as the night before's, but it is obvious that any attempt to create a cordial or remotely relaxed atmosphere is doomed. Of everyone, Geneviève is the most agitated. Long afterwards, Maigret will see her chest heaving with a woman's anger, or rather a lover's rage, since he could swear that is what she is feeling. She eats little and grudgingly. Not once does she look in Alban's direction, who, for his part, has stopped looking anyone in the eye.

He is just the sort of man to hoard every last scrap of paper, filing them and pinning them together in bundles like banknotes. He is also just the sort of man to cover his back given the remotest chance, even if it means leaving his companions in a tight spot.

All of this is palpable. There is something nasty in the air. Madame Naud is increasingly anxious. Naud, meanwhile, is doing his best to reassure his family, while possibly trying to accomplish something else in the process.

'By the way, I happened to see the prosecutor in Fontenay this morning. Incidentally, Alban, he's almost related to you on the distaff side because he married a Deharme, from Cholet.'

'The Cholet Deharmes are not related to the general's family. They're from Nantes and . . .'

'You know, inspector,' Naud went on, 'he was very reassuring. Of course he told my brother-in-law Bréjon that a preliminary investigation appeared inevitable, but apparently it will be purely formal, at least as far as we are concerned. I said you were here . . .'

Ah! He is already regretting blurting that out. Blushing slightly, he hurriedly takes a large mouthful of creamy lobster.

'What did he say about me?'

'He admires you a great deal. He has followed most of your investigations in the newspapers. Precisely because he admires you . . .' The poor man didn't know how to finish his sentence. '. . . He's surprised my brother saw fit to trouble a man like you over such a trivial matter . . .'

'I understand . . .'

'You're not upset? It's simply because he has such admiration . . .'

'Are you sure he didn't add that my involvement might give this affair an importance it doesn't warrant?'

'How do you know that? Have you seen him?'

Maigret smiles. What else can he do? He is just a guest, after all. Their hospitality has been faultless. Tonight's dinner is another minor masterpiece of traditional country cooking. And now, politely, and with a great deal of tact, they are giving him to understand that his presence threatens to harm his hosts.

There is a silence, as there was after the Alban incident. Madame Naud takes it upon herself to smooth things over, making a clumsier mess of it than her husband.

'I hope you'll stay on a few days anyway? After the fog, there'll most likely be a frost and you'll be able to take a few walks with my husband . . . Don't you think, Étienne?'

What a relief for everyone if Maigret were to reply, as they expect him to as someone with good manners, 'It would be delightful to stay, I've enjoyed your hospitality enormously, but alas, duty calls me back to Paris. Perhaps I will be driving by in the holidays . . . But, in the meantime, I will leave with wonderful memories, I can assure you . . .'

He does nothing of the sort. He eats without saying a word and, in his mind, calls himself a brute. These people have shown him nothing but kindness. Perhaps they do have the death of Albert Retailleau on their conscience, but hadn't the young man 'stolen their daughter's honour', as people of their kind would say? Had Madame Retailleau, the mother, lodged a complaint? Not a bit of it; she would be the first to say everything was for the best in the best of all worlds, wouldn't she?

There are three or four of them, perhaps more, trying to keep their secret, straining their every sinew, and the mere presence of Maigret must cause Madame Naud, for instance, intolerable suffering. When they were left alone earlier for a quarter of an hour, hadn't she been on the verge of screaming in agony by the end?

The whole thing is so simple! He can just leave the following morning with the entire family's blessing and, when he gets back to Paris, Examining Magistrate Bréjon will thank him with tears in his eyes!

If Maigret doesn't do so, is he solely motivated by a desire for justice? He wouldn't have dared look anyone in the eye and maintain as much. Cavre is part of the reason. As are the successive defeats Inspector Cadaver has inflicted on him since the previous evening, without sparing his former boss so much as a glance. He has come and gone as if Maigret didn't exist or were an entirely harmless adversary.

Wherever he goes, as if by magic testimonies melt away, witnesses don't remember anything or clam up, pieces of evidence like the cap vanish.

At last, after so many years, it is the turn of the luckless, the unlovely, the envious to win the day!

'What are you thinking about, inspector?'

He started:

'Nothing . . . I'm sorry . . . My mind sometimes wanders . . .'

To his embarrassment, he had piled his plate high without realizing. To put him at his ease, Madame Naud murmured, 'Nothing gives a hostess more pleasure than to see her cooking being appreciated. The fact Alban eats like a horse doesn't count; he'd eat any old thing. He's not a gourmet, he's a glutton.'

She was joking, but there was still a trace of rancour in her voice and eyes.

Finally Étienne Naud rejoined the conversation. Even

ruddier cheeked after a few glasses of wine, he ventured, toying with his knife, 'What about you, inspector, now you've had a little look around the town and asked a few questions, what's your view of it all?'

'He has got to know young Fillou,' his wife said, as if warning him of danger.

With the eyes of everyone on him, Maigret replied, enunciating every syllable, 'I think Albert Retailleau was unlucky . . .'

It didn't really mean anything, and yet Geneviève turned pale and was so struck by this inconsequential little remark that it seemed for a moment as if she were about to get up and leave. Naud was trying to make sense of it. Alban sneered, 'Now there's a remark worthy of a classical oracle. If, by amazing coincidence, I hadn't found proof that I was sleeping peacefully that night in a room in the Hotel de l'Europe eighty kilometres away, I wouldn't be easy in mind . . .'

'So you don't know,' Maigret retorted, 'that the police have a saying: the better a person's alibi, the more suspect he is?'

Groult-Cotelle bristled, taking the joke seriously.

'In that case you'll also have to suspect the prefect's private secretary of complicity, since he spent the evening with me. He's one of my childhood friends, and we meet up for the occasional dinner, which almost always goes on until two or three in the morning . . .'

What made Maigret take the pretence further? Was he provoked by this trumped-up aristocrat's blatant coward- ice? He took out his large notebook, so famous at the

Police Judiciaire, slipped off the elastic band and began questioning him in earnest:

'His name?'

'You really want me to tell you? As you wish. Musellier. Pierre Musellier. He has never married. He has a flat on Place Napoléon, above the Murs garage. It is fifty metres from the Hotel de l'Europe . . .'

'Shall we go and have coffee in the drawing room?' suggested Madame Naud. 'Will you pour, Geneviève? You're not too tired? You're looking pale, I think. Perhaps it would be better if you went to bed?'

'No.'

She was tense rather than tired. It was as if she had a score to settle with Alban, whom she did not take her eyes off.

'You returned to Saint-Aubin the following day?' asked Maigret, pencil in hand.

'The following day, yes. I got a lift with a friend to Fontenay-le-Comte. There, I had lunch with friends and, as I left, I happened to run into Étienne, who brought me back . . .'

'So, you go from friend to friend . . .'

He could not have said more explicitly that Alban was a sponger, which was the case. Everyone understood so clearly that Geneviève blushed and looked away.

'I still can't tempt you with one of my cigars, inspector?'

'May I know if my interrogation is over? In that case, I'll take the liberty of saying my goodbyes. I feel like getting home early tonight . . .'

'Perfect timing. I feel like a stroll into town. If you don't mind, we'll head off together.'

'I'm on my bicycle . . .'

'Not to worry. A bicycle can be wheeled, can't it? Besides, with the fog out there you might ride into the canal.'

What was going on? For one thing, when Maigret mentioned leaving with Alban Groult-Cotelle, Étienne Naud had frowned and seemed on the verge of saying he was coming with them. Did he think that Alban, who was obviously overwrought that evening, might be persuaded to confess? He gave him an insistent look, which clearly meant, 'For goodness' sake, be careful! You see the state you are in. He is more than a match for you . . .'

Similar, but harder, more contemptuous, was the girl's look, which said:

'At least try to have your wits about you!'

As for Madame Naud, she wasn't looking at anyone. She was worn out. Nothing made sense to her any more. She wouldn't be able to cope with the nervous tension for much longer.

But it was Alban himself who was behaving the most strangely. Unable to leave, he was hanging around the drawing room in what seemed like the hope of speaking to Naud.

'Didn't you ask me to look into your office about that insurance business?'

'Insurance – what do you mean?' Naud said without thinking.

'Doesn't matter. We'll talk about it tomorrow.'

What did he have to tell him that was so important?

'Are you coming, my dear sir?' insisted the inspector.

'You're sure you don't want me to drive you? If you'd like to take the car and drive yourself . . .'

'No, thank you. We're going to have a nice chat as we walk . . .'

The fog closed round them. Wheeling his bicycle with one hand and walking fast, Alban had to stop constantly because Maigret showed no inclination to keep up.

'Such good people. And what a close-knit family. Goodness, though, it must get dull here for a young girl at times. Has she got many friends?'

'Not that I know of here. Apart from her cousins, who come when the weather's warmer, or sometimes she goes and spends a week with them.'

'I suppose she also goes up to Paris to stay with the Bréjons?'

'She went there this winter actually.'

Maigret good-naturedly changed the subject. The two men could barely see one another in the whitish, freezing cloud that enveloped them. The station's electric glare looked like a lighthouse, and two other lights further off like boats out to sea.

'So, apart from a few trips to La Roche-sur-Yon, you hardly ever leave Saint-Aubin?'

'I sometimes go to Nantes, where I have friends, or Bordeaux, where my de Chièvre cousin is married to a ship-owner . . .'

'Paris?'

'I was there a month ago.'

'The same time as Mademoiselle Naud?'

'Possibly. I've no idea . . .'

They passed the two cafés facing one another and Maigret, stopping, suggested, 'What about a drink at the Lion d'Or? I am curious to see my former colleague Cadaver. A while ago at the station I saw a little fellow getting off a train and I have a hunch he is an associate who has been called in to help.'

'I'll say goodbye, then . . .' Alban said hastily.

'No, no. If you're not coming, I'll see you home. As long as you don't mind, that is?'

'To be perfectly frank, I'm looking forward to getting into bed. I suffer from painful headaches and I'm having an attack right now . . .'

'All the more reason to see you to your door. Does your maid sleep in the house?'

'Naturally.'

'I know people who prefer not to have their staff sleep under the same roof . . . Goodness! There's a light . . .'

'It's the maid.'

'She uses the drawing room? It's true that the room is heated. When you're not there, she does little sewing jobs, I suppose?'

They had stopped on the doorstep and, rather than knocking, Alban was searching for his key in his pocket.

'See you tomorrow, inspector! I daresay we'll run into one another at my friends, the Nauds . . .'

'Tell me . . .'

Alban was taking care not to open the door lest Maigret take it as an invitation to come in.

'It's stupid . . . I'm sorry . . . Can you believe it, nature calls, and since we're at your home . . . We men can be frank with one another, don't you think?'

'Come in. I'll show you the way . . .'

The passage was unlit, but the door to the drawing room on the left was ajar, casting a rectangle of light. Alban tried to usher Maigret along the passage, but the inspector opened the door all the way, as if involuntarily, and then stopped dead, crying, 'What on earth! My old pal Cavre! What are you doing here, dear friend?'

The former inspector had got to his feet, pale as usual, a sullen expression on his face. He gave Groult-Cotelle a withering glance, holding him responsible for the incident.

Alban was out of his depth. He tried to think of an explanation and, unable to come up with one, asked, 'Where's the maid?'

Cadaver was the first to regain his composure, saying with a bow, 'Monsieur Groult-Cotelle, I believe?' Alban didn't catch on immediately. 'I'm sorry to bother you at this hour. I just wanted a quick chat with you. The woman who let me in said you wouldn't be long, so . . .'

'That's enough!' growled Maigret.

'What?' Alban started.

'I said: that's enough!'

'What are you insinuating?'

'I'm not insinuating anything. Where is she, Cavre, this maid who showed you in here? There's no other light on in the house. In other words, she's asleep.'

'She told me . . .'

'For the second time, that's enough! No more play-acting! You can sit back down, Cavre. Well now, I see you've made yourself comfortable, taken off your coat, hung your hat on the coat rack. What were you busy reading?'

His eyes widened as he picked up the book lying near Cavre.

'*Perverse Pleasures*! Look at that! And you found this charming book here in our friend Groult's library, did you? . . . Tell me, gentlemen, why are you still standing there? Am I disturbing you? Don't forget your headaches, Monsieur Groult . . . You should take an aspirin.'

Alban retained enough presence of mind to retort, 'I thought nature called?'

'It's stopped, imagine that . . . So, my dear Cavre, how's the investigation? Tell me, just between us, you must have been sore when you found out I was involved, weren't you?'

'You're involved, are you? In what?'

'So it was Groult-Cotelle who sought out your talents, which, by the way, I am far from underestimating.'

'I'd never heard of Monsieur Groult-Cotelle before this morning.'

'Then it was Étienne Naud who told you about him when you met in Fontenay-le-Comte?'

'When you decide to submit me to a formal interrogation, inspector, I will be perfectly happy to answer all your questions in the presence of my lawyer.'

'If you were accused of stealing a cap, for instance?'

'For instance, yes.'

The drawing room was bathed in grey light because the bulb, which anyway was too weak for a room of that size, was grimy with dust.

'Perhaps I could offer you a drink?'

'Why not?' replied Maigret. 'As we've been thrown together like this . . . By the way, Cavre, that was one of your men I saw at the station just now, wasn't it?'

'That was one of my employees, yes.'

'Reinforcements?'

'If you like.'

'You had important matters to attend to tonight with Monsieur Groult-Cotelle?'

'I wanted to ask him some questions.'

'If it's about his alibi, you can set your mind at rest. He thought of everything. He even kept his bill from the Hotel de l'Europe.'

Cavre refused to be thrown. He had sat back down, crossing his legs and resting his morocco briefcase on top of them, and now waited, convinced, it seemed, that he would have the last word. Groult, who had filled three glasses with Armagnac, handed him one, which he refused.

'No, thank you. I only drink water.'

His abstemiousness had been the butt of enough jokes at the Police Judiciaire, unintentionally cruel ones, as it turned out, since Cadaver didn't refrain by choice but because of a severe liver complaint.

'And you, inspector?'

'Gladly!'

They fell silent. All three of them seemed to be playing a strange game of who could keep quiet the longest without backing down. Alban had drained his glass in one and poured himself a second. He was the only one still standing and from time to time he tucked in one of his books that was sticking out.

'Are you aware, sir,' Cavre finally said to him in a quiet voice, with icy composure, 'that you're in your own home?'

'What do you mean?'

'That you can entertain whomsoever you choose. I would have liked to speak with you without the inspector being present. If you prefer this gentleman's company to mine, I'm quite willing to withdraw and arrange another appointment.'

'In a word, the inspector is politely asking you to throw one of us out.'

'I don't understand, gentlemen! What's the point of this discussion? The simple fact is, I have nothing to do with this business. I was in La Roche when the boy died, as you know. Naturally I am a friend of the Nauds. I have spent a lot of time at their house. In a small town like ours, one can't choose who one knows.'

'Don't forget Saint Peter!'

'What do you mean?'

'That you'll have denied your friends, the Nauds, three times before the sun rises at this rate, assuming the fog lets it rise, that is.'

'It's all very well for you to joke. I'm still in an awkward position. I'm a regular guest of the Nauds; Étienne is my friend. You see, I don't deny it. What happened at their house? I have no idea, and I don't want to know. So I'm not the person you should be questioning about this matter.'

'Perhaps Mademoiselle Naud would be a better candidate, do you think? By the way, I don't know if you noticed her looking at you in a far from tender way this evening. I had the distinct impression she bore you a grudge.'

'Me?'

'Particularly when you handed me your hotel bill and made such an elegant attempt to cover your back. She didn't find that a very pretty sight at all. If I were you I'd be on your guard in case she tries to return the favour . . .'

Alban gave a hollow laugh.

'You're joking. Geneviève is a sweet child who . . .'

What made Maigret suddenly risk everything?

'Who's three months pregnant,' he said flatly, thrusting his jaw towards Alban.

'What . . . what are you saying?'

Cavre was similarly stunned. For the first time that day, he lost a little of his self-assurance and looked at his former boss with involuntary admiration.

'You didn't know, Monsieur Groult?'

'What are you trying to insinuate?'

'Nothing. I'm casting around . . . You want the truth as well, don't you? Well then, we're both casting around for it. Cavre has already got his hands on the bloodstained cap that is sufficient proof of the crime . . . Where is that cap, Cavre?'

Without answering, Cavre sank deeper into his chair.

'You'll pay dearly for the pleasure if you've destroyed it, I tell you . . . And now I feel I'm disturbing you. I'll leave you both. I imagine, Monsieur Groult-Cotelle, that I'll see you tomorrow at lunch with your friends, the Nauds?'

He went out. As the door was slammed shut behind him, he saw a skinny figure standing close by.

'Is that you, inspector?'

It was young Louis. Holed up behind the windows of the Trois Mules, he had no doubt seen the shadowy figures of Maigret and Alban go by. He had followed them.

'You know what they're saying, what everyone's going on about all over town?'

His voice shook with anxiety and indignation.

'People are saying *they* have got one over on you and that you're leaving tomorrow on the three o'clock train.'

And they had very nearly been right.

7. The Old Postmistress

As sometimes happened, some external factor seemed to be making Maigret more than usually sensitive at that moment. He had barely moved from Groult-Cotelle's doorway. He had taken a few steps in the dark and the fog that clung to his skin like a cold compress, with young Louis at his side, when he suddenly stopped.

'What's the matter, inspector?'

A thought had just struck Maigret and he was trying to follow its thread. He still registered the hubbub of voices, piercing but indistinct, that came through the shutters of the house. He also understood the teenager's alarm: he had stopped dead in the middle of the pavement for no apparent reason, like someone with heart problems who is halted in his tracks by an attack wherever he happens to be. It bore no relation to what was on his mind, nor was it of especial interest, but still he made a mental note: 'So, someone in Saint-Aubin has a weak heart . . .' And later, in fact, he was to learn that the previous doctor had died of angina pectoris. For years, people had seen him stop suddenly just like that in the middle of the street, standing rooted to the spot with a hand pressed to his heart.

Inside, they were having an argument or, at any rate, their yelling gave that impression. But Maigret wasn't really listening, unlike Louis Pockmarks, who, thinking he had worked out why the inspector had come to a standstill, was straining his ears conscientiously. The louder the voices, the less one could make out individual words. It sounded just like a record that has had a new, off-centre hole cut in it and blares out unintelligible sounds.

It wasn't the row that had broken out in the house between Inspector Cadaver and Alban Groult-Cotelle that had made Maigret stop so abruptly and seemingly stare off into space.

Just as he had stepped over the threshold, an idea had struck him. Not even an idea. It was vaguer than that, so vague that he was now trying to remember the feeling of it. Sometimes an insignificant incident – a barely notice-able smell, more often than not – takes us back for a split second to a moment in our lives. The sensation is so acute we're stunned, we want to cling on to that vivid recollec-tion of something we've experienced, but moments later it's gone and we can't even say what we were just thinking about. We rack our brains in vain and, for lack of answers to our questions, end up wondering if we hadn't actually recalled a dream or, who knows, a previous life.

It was just as the door was shutting. He was conscious of leaving the two embarrassed, furious accomplices to their own devices. They had something in common, those two men whom fate had brought together that night. You couldn't explain it rationally. Cavre was nothing like a bachelor. He was the quintessential cuckolded husband, seething with shame and pain. He reeked of envy, that emotion that can make a man look as corrupt as some hidden vices.

Maigret didn't really bear him a grudge. He pitied him, if anything. Naturally he had him in his sights and was determined to get the better of him, but he also felt a little sorry for this man who, when it came down to it, was nothing but a failure.

What was the link between Cavre and Alban? Something that links two entirely different but equally sordid things. It was almost a question of colour. They were both grey, greenish, both covered in moral and actual dust.

Cavre exuded hatred, whereas Alban Groult-Cotelle exuded fear and cowardice. Cowardice was the founding principle of his life. His wife had left him and taken his children. He hadn't tried to find them or bring them back; he probably hadn't even really suffered. He had selfishly made a new life for himself. Not being wealthy, he squatted in other peoples' nests, like a cuckoo. And if anything bad happened to his friends, he wasted no time leaving them in the lurch.

Maigret suddenly realized the trivial detail that had triggered these thoughts: it was the book he had found in Cadaver's hands when they had got to Alban's house, one of those grubby works of erotica that are sold under the counter in backrooms in Faubourg Saint-Martin . . .

Groult-Cotelle had those sorts of books in his library in the country . . . and Cavre had just happened unerringly to lay his hands on one!

But there had been something else, and that was what the inspector was trying to remember. For perhaps a tenth of a second, he had been lit up, so to speak, by a self-evident truth, but before he could grasp it, the flash of insight had vanished, leaving only the vaguest of impressions. And that was why he was standing stock-still like a cardiac patient trying to outwit his heart.

He was trying to outwit his memory. He was hoping . . .

'What's that light?' he broke off to ask.

They were both standing motionless in the fog. Some way off, Maigret could see a large, blurry halo of white light. He concentrated on this concrete detail to allow his intuition time to revive. He knew the little town now. So, what was over there where the light was shining, almost directly opposite Groult's house?

'Isn't that the post office?'

'It's the window next door,' replied Louis. 'The postmistress's window. She suffers from insomnia. She reads novels late into the night. Hers is always the last light to go out in Saint-Aubin . . .'

He kept an ear open for the raised voices. Groult-Cotelle was shouting the loudest, as if he refused to listen to reason at any price. Cavre's voice was deeper, more commanding.

Why did Maigret almost feel the urge to cross the street and press his face to that kitchen window, behind which the postmistress was doubtless reading? Was it intuition? Moments later the thought had gone out of his mind. He knew Louis was studying him anxiously, impatiently, wondering what could be going on in the great man's brain.

What had he sensed as he stepped over the threshold? Let's see . . . Paris was part of it . . . It was that book and the shops in Faubourg Saint-Martin selling books like it that had reminded him of Paris . . . Groult-Cotelle had gone to Paris . . . Geneviève Naud would have been there at the same time . . .

He saw the expression on her face when Alban had grotesquely produced his alibi. It wasn't just a look of disdain. Nor had she seemed like a girl at that moment either. She was a woman . . . a lover who was suddenly realizing how base her . . .

There, that was when the lightning had flashed across his mind and sadly vanished just as quickly. He was left with a vague sense of something despicable.

Yes, this business struck Maigret as very different now. Thus far he had considered it a purely bourgeois affair, an upper-middle-class family outraged to discover a kid without money or position in their daughter's bed. Had Naud killed him in a fit of rage? It was possible. He was close to pitying Naud, and especially Madame Naud. She knew everything and was desperately trying to remain silent, to master her terror. Every minute spent alone with the inspector was pure agony for her.

But now Étienne Naud and his wife receded into the background.

How did these thoughts fit together? Alban, that dusty, balding character, had an alibi. Was that really just a coincidence? Was it also just a coincidence that he had suddenly come across the bill from the Hotel de l'Europe?

No doubt he had really gone there. It needed checking but the inspector felt sure he had.

But why had he gone to La Roche-sur-Yon on that

particular evening? Was the prefect's private secretary expecting him?

'Needs checking!' growled Maigret.

He was still looking at the murky light of the post office. He still had his tobacco pouch in one hand and his pipe, which it hadn't occured to him to fill, in the other.

Albert Retailleau was furious . . .

Who had told him that? His companion, that's right, little Louis, the dead man's friend.

'Was he really furious?' the inspector suddenly asked.

'Who?'

'Your friend Albert. You told me that when he left you on that last evening . . .'

'He was very worked up. He knocked back a few brandies before going to see her.'

'He didn't say anything?'

'Wait . . . He said he didn't reckon he'd be staying around in this filthy town much longer.'

'How long had he been Mademoiselle Naud's lover?'

'I don't know . . . Wait . . . They weren't going together in midsummer. It must have started around October . . .'

'He wasn't in love with her before?'

'He didn't talk to her, at least . . .'

'Shh . . .'

Maigret had stopped moving and was listening intently. The voices had fallen silent. Instead, a noise was audible that struck the inspector.

'The telephone!' he said.

He had recognized the characteristic sound of country

telephones, with their handle you have to turn to call the post office operator.

'Run and look in the postmistress's window . . . You'll be quicker than me . . .'

He hadn't been mistaken. A second light went on in the window next to the first. The postmistress had gone into the post office, which only required her to step through a half-open door.

Maigret took his time. He was loath to run. Oddly enough, it was young Louis' presence that bothered him. He wanted to maintain a certain dignity in front of the kid. Finally he filled his pipe, lit it and slowly crossed the street.

'Well?'

'I *knew* she'd listen,' Pockmarks said under his breath. 'That old bag always listens. The doctor even complained to La Roche once, but she carries on regardless . . .'

They could see her, a diminutive figure dressed in black, with black hair and an ageless face. She had an earpiece in one hand, the answering jack in the other. The call must have just ended because she replaced the jacks and walked over to the light switch.

'You think she'd let us in?'

'If you knock on the little door round the back. Come this way. We'll go in through the yard.'

They squelched around in the pitch dark for a moment, threading their way between some tubs full of washing. A cat jumped off a rubbish bin.

'Mademoiselle Rinquet!' called the kid. 'Open up for a moment . . .'

'What is it?'

'It's me, Louis . . . Open up for a moment, please . . .'

As soon as she drew the bolt, Maigret hurriedly stepped inside for fear the door would be immediately shut again.

'No need to be afraid, mademoiselle . . .'

He was too tall and too burly for the kitchen, which was as minuscule as the postmistress herself. She had filled it with embroidered doilies and the sort of bone china and spun glass knick-knacks you find at fairgrounds.

'Groult-Cotelle has just made a telephone call.'

'How do you know?'

'He rang his friend Naud . . . You listened to the conversation.'

Caught out, she made a clumsy attempt to defend herself.

'But the post office is closed, monsieur. I'm not supposed to put through any more calls after nine o'clock . . . I do it all the same because I'm just next door and I like to be of service . . .'

'What did he say?'

'Who?'

'Look, if you don't answer me with a good grace, I'll have to come back tomorrow, officially this time, and write a report that will go through formal channels. What did he say?'

'There were two of them.'

'Talking at the same time?'

'Almost. Sometimes they'd both start. They'd try to drown each other out and after a while I couldn't understand a word . . . They must have each had an earpiece and been jostling each other in front of the telephone.'

'What were they saying?'

'Monsieur Groult said first: "Listen, Étienne, this can't go on. The inspector has just left. He came face to face with your man. I'm certain he knows everything and if you carry on . . ."'

'Well?' said Maigret.

'Wait . . . The other one butted in:

'"Hello . . . Monsieur Naud? Cavre here . . . It's obviously unfortunate that you couldn't find a way to detain him and prevent his finding me here, but . . ."

'"But I'm the one compromised here," yelled Monsieur Groult. "I've had enough, do you hear, Étienne? Manage by yourself from now on! Call your idiot of a brother-in-law and tell him he's finished making a hash of everything. In a sense, he is that wretched policeman's superior, so, since he sent him here, he'd better pull some strings and get him recalled to Paris . . . I'm warning you, if you put me in the same room as that man again, I . . ."

'"Hello! Hello! . . . " Monsieur Étienne cried in a panic at the other end of the line. "Are you still there, Monsieur Cavre? Alban is unnerving me . . . Is that really . . ."

'"Hello . . . It's Cavre here . . . Well, keep quiet then, Monsieur Groult . . . Let me get a word in . . . Stop pushing me . . . Is that you, Monsieur Naud? Yes . . . Well, there wouldn't be any danger if your friend Groult-Cotelle wasn't panicking . . . What? Should you call your brother-in-law? Well now, I would have advised against it a moment ago . . . No, he doesn't scare me . . ."'

The postmistress, who was getting a taste for this reconstruction, pointed at Maigret to clarify. 'He was talking about you, wasn't he? So, he said that you didn't scare him, but because Groult-Cotelle was a loose cannon . . . Shh . . .'

The telephone was ringing in the post office. The little old woman rushed in and switched on the light.

'Hello . . . What? . . . Galvani 17 98? I don't know . . . No, there shouldn't be a delay at this time of night . . . I'll call you back . . .'

Maigret recognized Bréjon's home number.

He looked at his watch. It was ten to eleven. Unless he had gone to the cinema or the theatre with his family, the examining magistrate would be in bed because it was common knowledge in the Palais de Justice that he was up by six every morning and studied his cases at dawn.

The jacks changed sockets.

'Is that you, Niort? . . . Will you put me through to Galvani 17 98? Line three is free? Give it to me, will you . . . Two was terrible just now . . . I'm fine, how are you? Are you working all night? What? No, you know I never go to bed before one in the morning . . . Yes, it's the same here . . . You can't see more than a couple of metres in front of your face . . . It'll be icy tomorrow morning . . . Hello! Paris? . . . Paris? Hello! Paris? Galvani 17 98? Come on, answer, dearie . . . Speak more clearly . . . Put me through to Galvani 17 98 . . . What? It's ringing? I can't hear anything . . . Let it ring . . . It's urgent . . . Ah yes, here's someone . . .'

She turned round, startled, as the bulky Maigret loomed over her, his hand outstretched, ready to grab her headset at the appropriate moment.

'Monsieur Naud? . . . Hello! . . . Monsieur Naud? Yes, I'm putting you through to Galvani . . . One second, it's ringing . . . Hold the line . . . Galvani 17 98? Saint-Aubin here . . . I'm connecting three . . . Go ahead, three . . .'

She did not dare protest as the inspector firmly took the headset from her and put it on his head. With a flourish, she inserted the answering jack in the socket.

'Hello! Is that you, Victor? What?'

There was static on the line and Maigret had the impression the examining magistrate was taking the call in bed. After his brother-in-law had said who was calling, he heard him repeat:

'It's Étienne . . .'

Presumably he was talking to his wife lying next to him.

'What? Is there any news? No? Yes? You're shouting too loud . . . It's making the receiver vibrate . . .'

Étienne Naud was one of those men who yell on the telephone as if they're permanently afraid of not being heard.

'Hello! . . . Listen, Victor . . . There's no news as such, no . . . I'll explain . . . I'll write you a letter too . . . Perhaps I'll come and see you in Paris in two or three days . . .'

'Speak more slowly . . . Give me a bit more room, Martha . . .'

'What did you say?'

'I told Martha to give me some more room . . . So? What's going on? Did the inspector get there all right? What do you think of him?'

'Yes . . . That's by the by . . . But I am calling about him . . .'

'Doesn't he want to look into your case?'

'No, he does . . . He's obsessed with it . . . Listen, Victor, you've got to find a way to get him back to Paris . . . No, I can't talk now . . . Knowing the postmistress . . .'

Maigret smiled as he looked at the little postmistress, who was bursting with curiosity.

'I'm sure you'll find a way . . . What? . . . It's difficult? It must be possible though . . . I assure you it's absolutely essential . . .'

It wasn't hard to imagine the examining magistrate frowning at his growing suspicions about his brother-in-law.

'It's not what you think . . . But he storms around, talking to everyone, doing more harm than good . . . Do you understand? At this rate, the whole town will be in turmoil and I'll be in an impossible position . . .'

'I don't know what to do . . .'

'Aren't you on good terms with his boss?'

'Yes . . . Obviously, I could ask the head of the Police Judiciaire . . . It's tricky . . . The inspector will find out about it sooner or later. He only agreed to go as a favour to me . . . Do you understand?'

'Do you want to get your niece – who's your god-daughter, let me remind you – into trouble, yes or no?'

'You think it's that serious?'

'Isn't that what I just said?'

Étienne Naud was clearly stomping his feet with impatience. Alban's panic had rubbed off on him, and the fact Cavre hadn't advised him against asking for Maigret to be recalled had done nothing to reassure him.

'Won't you put my sister on the line?'

'Your sister is in bed . . . I'm on my own downstairs . . .'

'What does Geneviève think?' The examining magistrate was clearly wavering, taking refuge in chit-chat. 'Is it raining there too?'

'I've no idea!' yelled Naud. 'I don't give a damn, do you hear? All that matters is that you get your confounded detective chief inspector to leave this house . . .'

'What in heaven's name is wrong?'

'What's wrong? What's wrong? What's wrong is that, if this goes on, we won't be able to stay here. He pokes his nose into everything, he never says a word, he . . . he . . .'

'All right, calm down. I'll try.'

'When?'

'Tomorrow morning . . . I'll see the head of the Police Judiciaire first thing, but I tell you, I don't like this. It's the first time in my career that . . .'

'But you'll do it, won't you?'

'I just said I would . . .'

'The telegram will probably get here around noon . . . He can take the three o'clock train . . . Make sure the telegram gets here in time.'

'Is Louise all right?'

'Yes, she's all right . . . Goodnight . . . Don't forget . . . I'll explain . . . Don't go imagining things, whatever you do . . . Say goodnight to your wife.'

The postmistress gathered from the expression on Maigret's face that the conversation had ended. She took back her headphones and switched the jacks around again.

'Hello? . . . Have you finished? . . . Hello, Paris . . . How

125

many calls? . . . Two? . . . Thank you . . . Goodnight, dear . . .'

And then, turning to the inspector who was putting his hat back on and relighting his pipe, she said, 'I could get the sack for less than that . . . So, do you think it's true?'

'What?'

'What people are saying . . . I can't believe that a man like Monsieur Étienne, who has everything a person could possibly need to be happy . . .'

'Good night, mademoiselle. Don't worry. I'll be discreet.'

'What were they saying?'

'Nothing interesting. Catching up on their families.'

'Are you going back to Paris?'

'Perhaps . . . Goodness me, I mean yes . . . There's every chance I'll be taking the train back tomorrow afternoon.'

He was calm now. He felt himself again. He was almost surprised to find the kid waiting for him in the kitchen. Louis was equally surprised to see a Maigret he hardly recognized; a Maigret who barely took any notice of him, who treated him offhandedly. 'Or could it be contempt?' thought the young man, hurt.

They found themselves outside, back in the darkness and fog, back in that absurdly small universe that was punctuated only by a few scattered lights.

'It was him, wasn't it?'

'Who . . . What?'

'Naud . . . He killed Albert.'

'I've no idea, son . . . It . . .'

Maigret stopped himself in time. He was going to say, 'It doesn't matter . . .'

That was what he was thinking or, more accurately, feeling. But he realized that the young man would be shocked if he said such a thing.

'What did he say?'

'Nothing very exciting . . . By the way, about Groult-Cotelle . . .'

They were walking towards the two inns. There were still lights on in them and, in one, figures were silhouetted like shadow puppets against the windows.

'Yes?'

'Has he always been a close friend of the Nauds?'

'Well . . . Not always, no . . . I was a small boy, you see? The house has been in his family for a long time, but when I was a kid and we'd go and play on the step, it was empty. I remember because we often used to climb into the cellar through a ventilator that didn't shut properly . . . Monsieur Groult-Cotelle was living with relatives then, who I think have got a chateau in Brittany . . . When he came back here, he was married . . . You should ask someone older than me . . . I must have been six or seven . . . I remember that his wife had a nice little yellow car which she drove herself. She'd often go off for drives on her own . . .'

'Did the couple see the Nauds?'

'No. I'm sure they didn't. I say that because I remember Monsieur Groult was always at the old doctor's house, who was a widower . . . I can see them by the window, playing chess . . . I may be wrong but I think his wife was the reason he didn't see the Nauds. They were friends before, because he and Naud went to school together.

They used to say hello in the street. I'd see them chatting on the pavement, but that was it . . .'

'So it was after Madame Groult-Cotelle left . . .'

'Yes. About three years ago. Mademoiselle Naud was sixteen or seventeen. She'd left school. She was at a boarding school in Niort for ages, and you only saw her one Sunday in four. The other reason I remember is because if you saw her any time other than the holidays, you always knew it was the third Sunday of the month . . . They became friends. Monsieur Groult spends half his time at the Nauds.'

'Don't they go on holiday together?'

'Yes, to Sables d'Olonne. The Nauds have had a villa built in Sables . . . Are you going back now? Don't you want to know if the private detective . . . ?'

The teenager looked in the direction of Groult's house, where a glimmer of light was still seeping through the shutters. Louis' idea of a police investigation probably bore little resemblance to Maigret's methods in this one. He was a little disillusioned, although he didn't dare show it.

'What did he say when you went in?'

'Cadaver? Nothing . . . No, he didn't say anything . . . Besides, it's not important . . .'

The inspector was far away, somewhere out of time as it were, and he answered his young companion half-heartedly, without really knowing what he was asking him.

At the Police Judiciaire they often used to joke about the Maigret that emerged at moments like this. He knew they talked about it behind his back too.

This Maigret seemed to swell out of all recognition, to become dense and heavy as if he were dead to the world or blind and dumb. A stranger or novice might easily mistake him for a sleepy, lumbering idiot.

'So, you're concentrating all your thoughts on the case, are you?' someone who fancied himself an expert in psychology had once asked him.

And he had replied with comic sincerity, 'I never think.'

It was almost true. He wasn't thinking now, for example, as he stood in the cold, wet street. He wasn't pursuing any particular idea. If anything, he was like a sponge.

The expression was Sergeant Lucas', who had worked on so many cases with him and knew him better than anyone.

'There's a moment in every investigation,' Lucas would relate, 'when the boss suddenly swells up like a sponge. It looks like he's filling up.'

Filling up with what, though? In his case, for instance, he was absorbing the fog and the darkness. He was no longer standing in the middle of just any old village. He wasn't just any old person who had ended up in those surroundings by chance.

Now he was almost like God the Father. He knew this village as if he had always lived there, or better still, as if he had created it. All the life going on in these small low houses hidden in the dark was familiar to him. He could see the men and women turning over in their warm, fusty beds and follow the thread of their dreams. A little light showed him a baby who was being given a warm bottle by its half-asleep mother. He felt the shooting pains of the invalid in the house on the corner. He foresaw the moment when the sleepwalking grocer would wake with a start.

He was in the café, sitting at its brown polished tables as the men shuffled their greasy cards and counted their red and yellow chips.

He was in Geneviève's room, suffering the torments of a lover's wounded pride with her. For that was what troubled her, the blows her pride had suffered. She had just endured what must have been the most painful day of her life, and who knew if she wasn't waiting for Maigret to come back so she could slip into his room again?

Madame Naud wasn't asleep. She was in bed but she wasn't asleep. In the darkness of her room, she listened to the sounds in the house, wondering why Maigret wasn't back yet and picturing her husband in the drawing room. Downstairs Étienne Naud sat waiting aimlessly, torn between the hope his telephone call had given him and the anxiety that increased the longer the inspector stayed away.

Maigret felt the heat of the cows in the barn, heard the mare kicking, pictured the old cook in a camisole . . .

Meanwhile at Groult's house . . . Look, a door was opening. Alban was showing his visitor out. He clearly loathed him. What else had he and Cavre said to each other in that dusty, stale-smelling drawing room after their telephone call to Naud?

The door closed again. Cadaver briskly walked off, his briefcase under his arm. He was pleased, although not unreservedly so. The game was almost won. He had defeated Maigret hands down. Tomorrow his old boss would be recalled to Paris. But he was a little humiliated not to have achieved this victory on his own. And then there was the inspector's threat about the cap, which preyed on his mind . . .

He headed off to the Lion d'Or, where his employee was waiting for him, putting away the brandy.

'Are you going back to where you're staying now?'

'Yes, son . . . What else am I going to do?'

'You're not giving up?'

'Giving up what?'

Maigret knew them all so well! How many other Pockmarks had he come across in his life, just as fervent, just as naive and knowing, flinging themselves at every obstacle in their paths, determined to achieve justice at all costs?

'It will pass, you know, little man,' he thought. 'In a few years you'll give a Naud or a Groult a nice low bow because you'll understand it's the wisest course of action when you're Fillou's son . . .'

What about Madame Retailleau, all alone in that house, where she had carefully hidden the notes in the soup tureen?

She had understood long ago. Doubtless she had been as good a wife as anyone else, as good a mother. She may not have been unfeeling, but she had learned that feelings are useless and had resigned herself. Resigned herself to fighting her corner with other weapons, to transforming all of life's accidents into hard currency.

Her husband's death had brought her her house and a pension that had allowed her to raise her son and give him an education.

Now Albert's death . . .

'I bet she wants a little house, in Niort rather than Saint-Aubin,' he muttered under his breath. 'A brand new, spotlessly clean little house . . . And a nice, secure little old age with the portraits of her husband and son looking down on her . . .'

As for Groult and his *Perverse Pleasures* . . .

'You're walking so fast, inspector . . .'

'Are you seeing me to the door?'

'Is that a bore for you?'

'Won't your mother worry?'

'Oh, she doesn't take any notice of me . . .'

There was regret as well as pride in his voice as he said that.

Come on, then! They had already passed the station and were heading down the boggy lane that ran alongside the canal. Old Désiré would be sleeping off his drink on his filthy mattress, while Josaphat, the postman, totted up his gains, preening himself on his brilliance and cunning . . .

Up ahead, at the end of the lane, where they could see what looked like the moon's halo behind a cloud, there was a large, cosy, peaceful house, one of those houses passers-by look at enviously and think how good it must be to live there.

'You can leave me now, son. We're here . . .'

'When will I see you again? Promise me you won't go without . . .'

'I promise . . .'

'You're really not going to give up?'

'I'm really not . . .'

If only! For Maigret was not thrilled by what he still had to do, and his shoulders sagged as he made for the steps. The door was open slightly. It had been left like that for him. There was a light on in the drawing room.

He sighed as he took off his heavy overcoat, which the fog had made heavier still, and remained standing on the mat for a moment to light his pipe.

'Come on, then!'

Torn between hope and mortal dread, poor Étienne was waiting for him in the chair Madame Naud had sat in that afternoon, suffering the same agonies.

On a side table stood a bottle of Armagnac, which appeared to have been put to good use.

8. Maigret Does a Maigret

There was nothing affected about Maigret's manner. He was cold, so he stood with his shoulders hunched and head cocked at an angle, like a thin-blooded person who always huddles by the stove. He had stayed out in the fog for a long time without thinking about the temperature and it was only when he took off his overcoat that he started shivering. Suddenly he became aware of all the freezing damp that had seeped into him.

He was sullen, as though he were coming down with flu, and uneasy, because the job ahead of him held little appeal. If that wasn't enough, he was also unsure. The time had come to bring matters to a head, and he suddenly found himself faced with two diametrically opposed courses of action, just when he had to make a definitive decision.

So when he entered the drawing room with a gruff air, blank eyes and a lurching, bear-like gait it was because he was thinking about all this, rather than cultivating the Maigret of legend.

He looked at nothing and took in everything, the glass and the bottle of Armagnac, the unnaturally sleek hair of Étienne Naud, who called out with forced joviality, 'Had a good night, inspector?'

Presumably he had just combed his hair. He kept a comb

in his pocket at all times, being particular about his appearance. But earlier, when he was waiting aimlessly on his own, he had probably been running his fingers feverishly through it.

Rather than reply, Maigret went to straighten a frame on the left-hand wall. That wasn't affectation either. He couldn't bear to see a picture hanging crooked on a wall. It irritated him, and he had no wish to be irritated by such a trivial thing when he was about to play his hand.

It was hot. Smells from dinner still hung in the air, to which the Armagnac added its aroma when the inspector finally poured himself a glass.

'There we are,' he sighed.

Naud started with surprise and anxiety. That 'There we are' sounded like the conclusion to an internal debate.

If he had been at police headquarters, or simply officially in charge of the case, Maigret would have felt obliged to stack all the odds in his favour and use traditional methods. Well, in the circumstances the traditional way would be to make Naud swing wildly between hope and fear, wear him down, panic him, reduce him to a state of absolute vulnerability.

It would be easy. Let him get tangled in his lies first. Then hazard some vague allusions to the two telephone calls. And finally, why not, say point-blank, 'Your friend Alban's going to be arrested tomorrow morning . . .'

But no, there would be none of that this time. Maigret simply went and leaned against the mantelpiece. The flames of the fire roasted his legs. Naud was sitting next to him. He probably still felt hopeful.

'I'll leave tomorrow at three o'clock as you want me to,' the inspector finally sighed after taking two or three hurried puffs on his pipe.

He pitied Naud. He felt embarrassed too. They were more or less the same age. This man's whole life had been orderly, comfortable and harmonious. Now he was risking everything, threatened with being locked up within a prison's four walls for the rest of his life.

Was he going to put up a struggle, carry on lying? Out of compassion, Maigret hoped not, the way you hope an animal that has been wounded by mistake will have a quick death. He avoided looking at him and stared at the carpet.

'Why do you say that, inspector? You know you're welcome here, and that my family both admires and likes you, as I do . . .'

'I heard your telephone conversation with your brother-in-law, Monsieur Naud.'

He put himself in the other man's shoes. It was one of those moments you hoped never to have to remember, so he pressed on. 'What's more, you were wrong about me. Your brother-in-law Bréjon asked me as a favour to come and help you in a delicate matter. Believe me, I realized right away that he had misunderstood you and that this wasn't the sort of help you were expecting. You wrote to him for advice in a moment of panic. You told him about the rumours, without saying, of course, that they were true. And in return, poor, honest, conscientious, by-the-book fellow that he is, he sent a detective to get you out of a tight spot.'

Naud struggled to his feet and walked over to the side

table, where he filled his glass to the brim with Armagnac. His hand was shaking. His forehead must have been beaded with sweat, but Maigret couldn't see. Even if he hadn't pitied him, a sort of tact would still have prevented him from looking at his host at that moment.

'I would have left the minute I got here, after our first conversation, if you hadn't employed Justin Cavre, and if that man's presence hadn't put me on my mettle.'

No denials from Naud, who was fiddling with his watch chain and staring at the portrait of his mother-in-law.

'Of course, as I'm not here in an official capacity, I'm not accountable to anyone. So you have nothing to fear from me, Monsieur Naud, and I feel all the more comfortable talking to you. The last few weeks have been a nightmare for you, haven't they? And for your wife, who I'm sure knows everything . . .'

Naud wasn't giving in yet. He had got to the point where it would only need a nod, a flicker of the eyelids, a muttered word for all the uncertainty to be over. Then he would be at peace. He could let go. Nothing to hide, no more games to play.

His wife must have been awake upstairs, listening intently, worried because there had been no sign of the two men turning in for the night. What about his daughter – had she been able to get to sleep?

'I'll speak my mind now, Monsieur Naud, and you'll understand why I didn't leave without saying anything, which, however strange it may seem to you, I was on the verge of doing. Listen carefully, take your time; I don't want you to misunderstand me. I have a very clear sense

– I am all but certain, in fact – that, guilty though you may be of Albert Retailleau's death, you are also a victim. I would go further. Your actions may have resulted in his death but you're not really responsible for it.'

And then it was Maigret's turn to go and pour himself a drink, to give his companion time to weigh his words. As Naud remained silent, he finally looked him full in the face, forced him to meet his gaze and asked, 'Don't you trust me?'

The result was as painful as it was unexpected, for Naud's surrender took the form of a fit of weeping. The grown man's eyes swelled, clouded over, swam with tears. His lips stuck out in a childish pout. He fought it for a moment, standing uneasily in the middle of the drawing room, then finally rushed over and leaned against the wall, his head buried in his arms, his shoulders heaving spasmodically.

There was nothing to do but wait. Twice Naud tried to speak, but it was too soon, he hadn't regained enough composure. Maigret had discreetly sat down by the fireplace, and was rearranging the logs with the tongs rather than poking the fire, as he would usually have done.

'In a moment,' Maigret said finally, 'you can tell me exactly what happened, if you like. Not that there's any great need, at least as far as the events of that night are concerned; they're easy to reconstruct. Other sequences of events are a different matter . . .'

'What do you mean?'

Naud was as tall and strong as ever, but he seemed insubstantial all of a sudden, as if he had been hollowed out. He was like one of those children prone to sudden growth spurts who have the height and build of a grown man when they're only twelve.

'You never suspected your daughter was involved with this young man?'

'I didn't even know him, inspector! I mean, I knew he existed because I know more or less the whole village, but I wouldn't have been able to put a name to the face. I still wonder where Geneviève, who hardly ever went out, could have met him . . .'

'You were in bed next to your wife?'

'Yes . . . And you see . . . It's ridiculous . . . We'd had goose for dinner . . .'

He clung to details of this kind as if, by giving the truth a veneer of familiarity, they made it less tragic.

'I like goose, although it's hard on my digestion. About one in the morning, I got up to take some bicarbonate of soda. You know the layout of the house pretty much. After my bedroom comes my dressing room, then a guest bedroom, then a room we never go into because . . .'

'I know . . . In remembrance of a child . . .'

'Finally there's my daughter's room, which as a result is off on its own. Both the maids, you see, sleep on the floor above . . . So, I was in my dressing room. I was groping about in the dark because I didn't want to wake my wife, who would have told me off for being greedy. I heard a hum of voices. People were arguing in the house. I didn't think for a moment that the noise could be coming from my daughter's room . . .

'But once I was in the passage, I had to face facts. Besides, there was a light under her door. I recognized a man's voice . . .

'I don't know what you would have done in my place, inspector. I don't know if you have a daughter. We're still quite old-fashioned here in Saint-Aubin. Perhaps I'm especially naive. Geneviève is twenty. Well, it had never occurred to me that she could hide anything from her mother and me! As for thinking that a man . . . No! You see, even now . . .'

He rubbed his eyes and mechanically took a pack of cigarettes out of his pocket.

'I almost rushed in in my nightshirt. I'm old-fashioned that way too and I still wear nightshirts rather than pyjamas. At the last minute I realized how ridiculous I looked, went back into my dressing room and got dressed, still without turning on the light . . . As I was putting on my socks, another sound struck me, outside this time. The dressing-room shutters weren't closed; I pulled back the curtain. There was a moon, and I could see the figure of a man climbing down from my daughter's room into the yard on a ladder . . .

'I put on my shoes, God knows how . . . I rushed down the stairs . . . I wasn't sure, but I thought I heard my wife's voice calling, "Étienne . . ."

'Have you ever been curious enough to look at the key to the door to the yard? It's an old key, huge, a real hammer . . . I couldn't swear to you that I picked it up by accident, and yet it wasn't premeditated either, because I hadn't planned to kill him and, if you'd told me at that moment . . .'

His voice was low but shaking. To calm himself, he lit a cigarette and took several long drags like a condemned man.

'The man went round the house and climbed the low wall by the lane. I followed him, without it occurring to me to muffle the sound of my steps. He must have heard me and yet he walked on unhurriedly. When I wasn't far away, he turned and, without seeing his face, I felt, I don't know why, that he was taunting me.

'"What do you want from me?" he asked in an aggressive, contemptuous voice.

'I swear, inspector, there are moments in your life you wish you've never lived through. I recognized him. As far as I was concerned, he was just a boy. But that boy had come out of my daughter's bedroom and was goading me. I didn't know what to do. Things like that don't happen the way you imagine. I shook him by the shoulders without finding the words to say what I wanted, and he shouted in my face:

'"You hate it that I'm breaking it off with your bitch of a daughter! . . . You were all in on it, weren't you?"'

He ran his hand over his face.

'I don't know, inspector. With the best will in the world I couldn't tell you exactly what happened. He was as furious as I was, but he was more in control. He was the one insulting me, insulting my daughter . . . Instead of falling on his knees at my feet, as I'd perhaps stupidly imagined he would, he mocked me, my wife, this house. He said things like, "Oh yes, such a lovely family!"

'He used the foulest language about my daughter, words I can't repeat, and then I don't know what happened, I started hitting him. I had the key in my hand. The boy's reaction caught me by surprise. He headbutted me in the stomach and the pain was so bad that I started to hit harder . . . He fell . . .

'I ran off at first, tried to go home . . . I swear that all this is the truth . . . I thought I'd call the Benet gendarmerie. As I got near the house I saw a light in my daughter's room. I thought if I told the truth. You can understand, though. I retraced my steps . . . He was dead . . .'

'You carried him on to the train track,' said Maigret, to help him and to get this depressing explanation over with more quickly.

'Yes . . .'

'By yourself?'

'Yes . . .'

'And when you got back?'

'My wife was standing by the front door. She whispered, "What have you done?"'

'I tried to deny it, but she'd realized. She looked at me with a mixture of terror and pity. I was in a sort of feverish state, so while I got into bed, she sat in the dressing room, checking my clothes one by one to make sure that . . .'

'I understand.'

'You may not believe it, but since then neither my wife nor I have had the strength to talk to our daughter about this. Not a single word has passed between us on the subject. Not one allusion. That might be the most terrible thing of all. Sometimes it's unbelievable. Life goes on in this house just as it always has, but the three of us know . . .'

'And Alban?'

'I can't explain . . . I didn't think about him at first. Then, the following day I was surprised not to see him come through the door as we sat down to eat. I started talking about him, just to have something to say. I said: "I must call Alban." I did, and his maid said he wasn't home. But I was sure I heard his voice in the background when she picked up the telephone . . .

'It became an obsession for me. Why hasn't Alban come to see us? Does Alban suspect anything? It's stupid to admit, but I got to the point of thinking Alban was the only danger, and four days later, when he still hadn't set foot in the house, I went to see him.

'I wanted to know the reason for his silence. I hadn't intended to talk but I ended up telling him everything. I needed him. You'd understand if you were in my position. He told me what people in town were saying. He described the funeral . . .

'I heard people were beginning to suspect me, and then another idea started going round my brain and I couldn't stop it: I should atone for what I'd done . . . Don't smile, I beg you . . .'

'You are the latest in a long line, Monsieur Naud!'

'Did the long line, as you put it, all behave as idiotically as me? One fine day did they take it upon themselves to go and see the victim's mother? Because that's what I did, melodramatically, under the cover of darkness, after Groult had made sure there was no one on the roads . . . I didn't come right out and confess the truth to her . . . I said that it was a terrible tragedy; that, as a widow, she had no one to support her now . . .

'I don't know whether she's an angel or a demon, inspector. I can still see her with her pale face, standing perfectly still by her fireplace, a shawl over her shoulders. I had two bundles of twenty-thousand-franc notes in my pocket. I didn't know how to take them out, put them on the table. I was ashamed of myself. I was . . . yes, I was ashamed of her too . . .'

'But still the money went from my pocket on to the table.

'"Every year, madame, I will consider it my duty . . ."

'She frowned, so I added hastily, "Unless you'd rather I made a single deposit in your name . . ."'

He fell silent, so oppressed he had to go and pour himself another glass of Armagnac.

'There it is . . . I was wrong not to come right out immediately and confess . . . Afterwards it was too late . . . Outwardly everything in the house was the same . . . I don't know how Geneviève had the strength to carry on as if nothing had happened, and there have been times when I've wondered if it wasn't all an illusion . . .

'I realized some people in the village suspected me, then I started to get anonymous letters. I knew that others had been sent to the public prosecutor's office. I wrote to my brother-in-law, like an idiot, because what could he do, especially when he didn't know the truth? I vaguely thought that examining magistrates could cover up scandals, that's the sort of thing you hear people say . . .

'Instead, he sent you here just when I'd written to a private detective agency in Paris . . . Oh yes, I did that too! I picked one blind from a newspaper advertisement!

144

I'd rather have died than confide in my brother-in-law but I told a complete stranger because I was desperate for reassurance . . .

'He knew you were on your way . . . I cabled the Cavre agency immediately after my brother-in-law had said when you'd be arriving . . . We arranged to meet the following day in Fontenay . . .

'What else do you want to know, inspector? How you must despise me! . . . Of course you do! And I despise myself too, I can assure you. Of all the criminals you've come across, I bet you've never known one as stupid . . .'

Maigret smiled for the first time. Étienne Naud was sincere. His despair wasn't remotely put on. And yet, as with all criminals, to use his word for it, his attitude suddenly revealed a certain pride.

He was annoyed and humiliated *to have made such a wretched job of his wrongdoing!*

For a few seconds, a few minutes even, Maigret sat perfectly still, staring at the flames gnawing the blackened logs. Thrown by this reaction, Étienne Naud didn't know where to put himself and stood hesitantly in the middle of the room, his mind racing.

After all, given that he had confessed everything, given that he had voluntarily humiliated himself, wasn't it natural to think the inspector would be more considerate, give him some moral support?

Hadn't he dragged himself through the dirt? Hadn't he painted a pathetic picture of his and his family's sufferings?

Moments earlier, before he confessed, he had had the impression Maigret was moved by his predicament and inclined to be more so. He had counted on that sympathy.

But now every trace of it seemed to have vanished. The scene had played itself out, and the inspector was calmly smoking his pipe, his gaze revealing nothing but cold, intense concentration.

'What would you do in my place?' Naud ventured again.

A look made him think he might be going too far, like a child who has been forgiven for doing something wrong and takes advantage of this leniency to be even more demanding and unbearable than ever.

What was Maigret thinking? Naud was beginning to suspect his attitude might just have been a trap. He almost expected to see him stand up, take a pair of handcuffs out of his pocket and utter the ritual words, 'In the name of the law . . .'

'I wonder . . .'

It was Maigret who was hesitating now, still puffing at his pipe, crossing and uncrossing his legs.

'I wonder . . . yes . . . whether we mightn't ring your friend Alban? What time is it? Ten minutes past midnight. The postmistress shouldn't be in bed yet, she'll put us through . . . Well, yes, let's do that then . . . If you're not too tired, Monsieur Naud, I think we'd better get this all over and done with tonight so I can catch my train tomorrow . . .'

'But . . .'

He couldn't find the words, or rather he didn't dare pronounce the ones that were on the tip of his tongue: 'But isn't it all over and done with?'

'Do you mind . . . ?'

Maigret crossed the drawing room, went into the hall and turned the handle of the telephone.

'Hello . . . I'm sorry to disturb you, my dear mademoiselle . . . It's me, yes . . . You recognized my voice? No, no . . . No trouble at all . . . Would you be kind enough to put me through to Monsieur Groult-Cotelle, please? Let it ring for a long time, in case he's fast asleep . . .'

Through the half-open door, he saw Étienne Naud looking completely at a loss. He seemed to have lost all his nerve and fibre. Resigned to his fate, he was philosophically downing a mouthful of Armagnac.

'Monsieur Groult-Cotelle? How are you? You were in bed . . . What's that? You were reading in bed? Yes, it's Detective Chief Inspector Maigret here . . . I'm at your friend's house, yes . . . We are having a chat . . . What? You've caught a cold? That's inconvenient . . . It's as if you'd guessed what I was going to say . . . We'd like you to drop round . . . Yes . . . The fog, I know . . . You'd got undressed? . . . In that case, we will come and see you . . . It won't take us a minute in the car . . . What? You'd rather come here? No . . . Nothing in particular . . . I'm leaving tomorrow . . . Surprising as it may seem, I have been called back to Paris on important business . . .'

Poor Naud was still more confused. He was staring at the ceiling, doubtless thinking that his wife could hear everything. She would be distraught. Perhaps he should go and reassure her – but how could he? Maigret no longer inspired him with confidence. He was beginning to regret his confession.

'What's that? A quarter of an hour? Too long . . . Get here as quickly as possible . . . See you right away . . . Thank you . . .'

The inspector may have been play-acting. Was it so urgent or was he reluctant to spend the next ten minutes or quarter of an hour in a tête-à-tête with Étienne Naud in the drawing room?

'He's coming,' Maigret announced. 'He's very worried. You can't imagine the state my telephone call put him in . . .'

'But he has no reason to . . .'

'You think?' Maigret asked simply.

Naud was increasingly bewildered.

'Do you mind if I get a bite to eat from the kitchen? Don't trouble . . . I can find the switch . . . I know where the refrigerator is . . .'

He turned on the light. The range was out. He found a chicken leg glazed with sauce. He cut a thick slice of bread and buttered it.

'Tell me . . .'

He came back into the drawing room, eating.

'There isn't any beer in the house, is there?'

'You wouldn't rather a glass of Burgundy?'

'I feel like beer, but if you don't have any . . .'

'There should be some still in the cellar . . . I always order a few cases, but as we hardly ever drink it, I don't know if . . .'

Just as after the most poignant bereavements a family will interrupt their weeping for a moment in the middle of the night to have something to eat, so, after the drama of

148

the past hour, the two men matter-of-factly went down to the cellar.

'No . . . This is lemonade . . . Wait . . . The beer must be under the stairs . . .'

And so it was. They went back upstairs with bottles under their arms. Next, large glasses had to be found. Maigret carried on eating, holding the chicken leg in his fingers, his chin greasy with sauce.

'I wonder if your friend Alban will come on his own,' he said casually.

'What do you mean?'

'Nothing. Let's have a bet . . .'

There was no time, however. Someone tapped on the front door. Étienne Naud hurried out, while Maigret, with his beer, bread and chicken, took up position in the middle of the drawing room.

He heard a hum of voices:

'I took the liberty of bringing this gentleman whom I met on the way and who . . .'

Maigret's eyes hardened for a second, then instantly lit up with a fierce glee as he called out:

'Come in, Cavre! I was expecting you . . .'

9. *A Noise Behind the Door*

Dreams that apparently only last a few seconds can leave their mark on us for a long time, sometimes our whole lives. Similarly, for a split second, the characters who came into the drawing room struck Maigret as entirely different from how they were, or at any rate from how they believed themselves to be. That was how they would live on in the inspector's memory.

They were all roughly the same age, including Maigret, and as he looked at them in turn, he felt a little as if he were with a group of boys in their last year at school.

Étienne Naud must have been just as burly and chubby when he took his baccalaureate as he was now, with the same sturdy but mild air, the same good manners and hint of shyness.

Cavre the inspector had met when he was only just out of school, and he was an irascible loner even then. He was vain in those days but, no matter how hard he tried, clothes never looked the same on him as they did on other people. Permanently shabby and dishevelled, he cut a sad figure. His mother must have spent her whole time when he was a boy saying, 'Go on, Justin, go and play with the others . . .'

And no doubt she used to confide in her neighbours, 'My son never plays. I worry about his health. He's too clever. He's always thinking . . .'

As for Alban, he bore a striking resemblance to his younger self: those long, thin legs, that elongated, vaguely aristocratic face, those long pale hands with their scattering of reddish hair, that upper-class elegance . . . He must have copied his chums' essays, scrounged their cigarettes, told them smutty jokes in the corner.

And yet here they were in deadly earnest, implicated in an affair that could see one of them locked up for the rest of his life. They were grown men. Somewhere in the world two children were walking around with Groult-Cotelle's name and, who knew, some of his flaws too. Upstairs, there was a woman and a girl who wouldn't sleep a wink that night. As for Cavre, he must be brooding over what his wife would be getting up to while he was away.

It was strange. Étienne Naud had come right out and confessed his crime to Maigret, admitting his most secret fears to him, man to man. But now he was blushing to the roots of his hair as he showed the newcomers into the drawing room and vainly trying to appear nonchalant.

There was something childish about his embarrassment. For a few seconds, it was as if Maigret had become a schoolmaster or professor. Naud had been left alone with him to be questioned about a misdemeanour and reprimanded. Now his chums were coming back into the room and looking inquiringly at him as if to say, 'How did you bear up?'

Well, he had borne up badly. He hadn't held his own. He had started crying. He wondered if there were traces of tears on his cheeks and eyelids.

He would have liked to put on a swagger, convince them everything had gone fine. He bustled about, fetching glasses from the sideboard in the dining room and pouring out generous measures of Armagnac.

Did the inspector take his cue from these echoes of a time in our lives when our actions are yet to have any consequences? He waited until everyone had sat down, then came and planted himself in the middle of the drawing room. He looked at Cavre and Alban in turn, then said bluntly, 'Well, gentlemen, it's over!'

Only then, for the first time since he had become involved in this affair, did he do a Maigret, as they said in the Police Judiciaire when an inspector tried to imitate the big boss. With his pipe clenched between his teeth, his hands in his pockets and his back to the fire, he held forth, his voice sometimes dropping to a growl. He jabbed at the logs with the tongs, then went from one to the other with his heavy, bear-like gait, asking a question or suddenly falling unnervingly silent.

'Monsieur Naud and I have just had a long, amicable conversation. I told him that I had decided to go back to Paris tomorrow so it would be better all round, before we parted company, if we told each other the truth. And that is what we did. Why do you start like that, Monsieur Groult? By the way, Cavre, my apologies for bringing you out just when you were about to go to bed. Yes, I'm the guilty party. I knew very well when I rang our friend Alban that he wouldn't have the nerve to come by himself. I wonder why he felt threatened by my invitation to come and have a chat with us . . . Anyway, he had a private detective to hand, and, much as he would have wished to bring a lawyer, he settled for second best . . . Isn't that so, Groult?'

'It wasn't me who sent to Paris for him!' retorted the balding would-be gentleman.

'I know. It wasn't you who battered the hapless Retail-leau to death, since, as chance would have it, you were in La Roche at the time. It wasn't you who left your wife, since she left you. It wasn't you ... Fundamentally, you see, you are a negative creature ... You have never done anything good in your life ...'

Worried at finding himself in the hot seat like this, Groult-Cotelle called Cavre to his assistance, but, with his leather briefcase on his lap, the private detective was looking uneasily at Maigret.

He knew the police, and the boss in particular, well enough to understand that Maigret had engineered this scenario with a specific aim in mind. By the end of their little get-together the case would be resolved one way or another.

Étienne Naud hadn't protested when the inspector said, 'It's over!'

So what else did Maigret want? He was roaming about, planting himself in front of one or other of the portraits, pacing from door to door, talking constantly as if he were improvising. Cavre found himself wondering if he wasn't playing for time. Was he waiting for something he thought should already have happened?

'So, I'm leaving tomorrow, as you all want me to. By the way, I ought to give you a piece of my mind for not trusting me more – you especially, Cavre, since we know each other. For goodness' sake, you knew I was just a guest, who was being treated as well as anyone could possibly expect.

'What happened in the house before I got here was none

of my concern. You could have at least asked me for advice, couldn't you? After all, what was Naud's situation? He had done something unfortunate, very unfortunate even. But had anyone lodged a complaint? No. The young man's mother was satisfied, if I may put it like that . . .'

And then, with a lightness that deceived them all, Maigret deliberately said this terrible sentence:

'The only people involved were respectable folk, people of breeding. There were rumours, of course. You may have been alarmed by one or two disagreeable pieces of evidence, but our friend Cavre's diplomacy and Naud's money, together with certain people's weakness for drink, averted that danger. As for the cap, which incidentally is not in itself conclusive proof, I presume Cavre took care to destroy it. Isn't that so, Justin?'

The latter gave a start as he heard himself addressed by his first name. Everyone turned to him, but he avoided answering.

'So that's where we were, or rather where our host was. Anonymous letters were going round. The prosecutor and the police had been sent some. An investigation was in the offing. What do you advise your client, Cavre?'

'I'm not a legal adviser.'

'That's your modesty speaking, I must say! If you want to know what's on my mind, I'll tell you right now, and it won't be an opinion, because I'm not a lawyer either. I think that in a few days Naud will feel the need to go travelling with his family. He is rich enough to sell his business and move elsewhere, abroad perhaps . . .'

Naud gave a sigh that sounded more like a sob at the

thought of leaving what had been his whole life up until then.

'That only leaves our friend Alban . . . What are your plans, Monsieur Alban Groult-Cotelle?'

'You don't have to answer,' Cavre put in hastily as he saw him opening his mouth. 'I should add that we're under no obligation to put up with this interrogation. Which, in any case, is not really one at all. If you knew the inspector as I do, you'd know he's putting on an act. He's trying his singing lesson, as they say at Quai des Orfèvres. I don't know if you have made a confession, Monsieur Naud, nor by what means it was extracted from you. But what I am certain of is that my former colleague has a specific aim in mind. I cannot make out what it is yet, but, whatever it is, I am warning you against it.'

'Well said, Justin!'

'I don't need your opinion.'

'I'm giving it anyway.'

And then Maigret abruptly changed his tone. The thing he had been waiting for for over a quarter of an hour, which had compelled him to put on this piece of theatre, had finally just happened. It wasn't pure fancy that had made him roam about, constantly pacing from the hall door to the one leading to the dining room.

Nor was it even hunger or greed that had made him go into the kitchen earlier to get some bread and a piece of chicken. He needed to know if there was another staircase besides the one leading down to the hall. There was: a staff staircase by the kitchen.

When he had telephoned Groult-Cotelle, he had spoken

in a very loud voice, as if he were unaware that two women were supposedly asleep in the house.

Now there was someone behind the half-open dining-room door.

'You're right, Cavre, for, however sad a person you may be, you're no fool . . . I have an aim in mind, and that aim, I'll come right out with it, is to prove that Naud is not really the guilty party . . .'

No one was more astonished than Étienne Naud, who had to stop himself exclaiming aloud. Alban, meanwhile, had turned pale and, something Maigret hadn't noticed about him before, his forehead had come out in little red blotches, as if a sudden attack of nettle rash had revealed his internal turmoil.

It reminded the inspector of a murderer of some notoriety who, after holding his own for twenty-eight hours of questioning, had suddenly had an accident in his trousers like a scared child. Maigret and Lucas, who were interrogating him, had smelled it and looked at one another. From that moment on, they had known the game was up.

Alban Groult-Cotelle's nettle rash was similar, and the inspector had trouble suppressing a smile.

'Tell me, Monsieur Groult, would you rather tell us the truth or would you like it to come from me? Take your time. Naturally you have my permission to consult your lawyer . . . Justin Cavre, I mean. Feel free to go off into a corner if you want to agree on a plan of action . . .'

'I have nothing to say . . .'

'So it's up to me to inform Monsieur Naud, who is entirely in the dark, why Albert Retailleau was killed, is it?

For, strange as it may seem, although Étienne Naud knows *how* the young man was killed, he has absolutely no idea *why* he was . . . What do you say to that, Alban?'

'You're lying!'

'How can you claim I'm lying when I haven't said anything yet? Come now! I'll ask another question and it will come to the same thing. Will you tell us why on a certain, very specific day you suddenly felt the need to go to La Roche-sur-Yon and make sure you returned with your hotel bill?'

Still baffled, Étienne Naud looked anxiously at Maigret, convinced he was making matters worse. Moments earlier he had been impressed by the inspector, but Maigret was rapidly losing prestige in his eyes. This hounding of Groult-Cotelle made no sense; it was becoming hateful.

So much so that Naud intervened, as an honourable man who refuses to see an innocent man unjustly accused, a host who will not allow one of his guests to be dragged over the coals.

'I assure you, inspector, you are on the wrong track . . .'

'I am sorry to have to disabuse you, my dear sir, especially because what you are about to hear will be extremely unpleasant. Won't it, Groult?'

The latter had sprung to his feet and looked for a moment as if he were about to hurl himself at his tormentor. He had the utmost difficulty controlling himself, clenching his fists and trembling all over. Finally he made as if to head for the door.

Maigret stopped him with a little question, asked in the most innocent way possible:

'Going upstairs?'

Who would have guessed, seeing Maigret so heavy-set and stubborn, that he was sweating as much as his victim? His shirt stuck to his back. He was straining to hear. The truth was, he was afraid.

A few minutes earlier, he was certain Geneviève was listening behind the door, as he had hoped she would be. It had been for her benefit that he had spoken in such a loud voice when he was on the telephone to Groult-Cotelle in the hall.

'If I'm right,' he had thought, 'she'll come down-stairs . . .'

And she had. Or at least, he had heard a slight rustle in the dining room and the door had moved a little.

The tone he had taken with Groult-Cotelle had been for Geneviève's sake too. But now he was wondering if she was still there because he couldn't hear anything any more. He thought she might have fainted, but there hadn't been any sound of a fall.

He was searching desperately for an opportunity to look behind that half-open door.

'Going upstairs?' he had asked Alban.

And the latter, unable to take it any more, retraced his steps and drew himself up to his full height only centimetres away from his enemy.

'What are you insinuating? Tell me! What fresh slanders are these? There isn't a word of truth in what you're going to say, you hear?'

'Look at your legal adviser!'

Cavre's face wore a crestfallen expression, because he

realized that Maigret was on the right track, and that his client was trapped.

'I don't need anyone's advice. I don't know what stories you've heard or who told you them. But I want to say before you start that they're lies and if some people's minds have . . .'

'You are vile, Groult.'

'What?'

'I say you're a revolting character. I say, and I will keep on saying, that you are truly responsible for the death of Albert Retailleau and that if human justice were perfect, life imprisonment would be too good for you. Personally, although this is something I rarely feel, I would take pleasure in walking you to the foot of the guillotine . . .'

'Gentlemen, I call you to witness . . .'

'Not only did you kill Retailleau but you killed other people as well . . .'

'Me? Me? . . . You're mad, inspector . . . He's mad. I swear he's raving mad . . . Where are they, these people I killed? Do show them to me, please . . . Well, we're waiting, Sherlock Holmes . . .'

He laughed mockingly. His agitation had reached fever pitch.

'Here's one for a start,' Maigret replied quietly, pointing at Étienne Naud, who had no idea what was happening.

'He strikes me, as they say, as a dead man in excellent health. If all my victims . . .'

Alban had gone up to Maigret with such a show of arrogance that the response was automatic: the inspector's hand literally flew out and landed with a dull thwack on his livid cheek.

They might have come to blows, grappling with one another and rolling around on the carpet like the teenagers the inspector had been thinking of earlier, if they hadn't heard a frightened voice at the top of the stairs.

'Étienne! . . . Étienne! . . . Inspector! . . . Quick! . . . Geneviève.'

It was Madame Naud calling, as she took a few more steps down the stairs. She was astonished they hadn't heard her because she had been calling for a while.

'Quick, go upstairs . . .' Maigret said, addressing Naud, 'to your daughter's room . . .'

And then, looking Cavre squarely in the eye, he said in a tone that brooked no contradiction, 'As for you, don't let him go . . . Understand?'

He followed Étienne Naud up the stairs and they both reached the girl's bedroom at the same time.

'Look . . .', moaned Madame Naud, panic-stricken.

Geneviève was lying across her bed, fully dressed. Her eyes were half-open but glassy, like a sleepwalker's. A tube of Veronal lay in pieces on the rug.

'Help me, madame . . .'

The hypnotic was only starting to take effect, and the girl was still half-conscious. She recoiled, horrified, as the inspector went over, grabbed hold of her and unclenched her teeth.

'Get me water, lots of it, hot if you can . . .'

'Go on, Étienne, you do it . . . In the boiler . . .'

Poor Étienne hurried off, bumping into the walls of the passage and the servants' staircase like a cockchafer.

'Don't worry, madame . . . We're in time . . . It's my

fault, I didn't imagine she'd react like this . . . Give me a handkerchief, a towel, anything . . .'

Less than two minutes later, the girl had vomited profusely and was sitting limply on the edge of her bed, obediently drinking the water the inspector kept giving her to make her vomit again.

'You can ring the doctor. He won't do much, but just to be on the safe side . . .'

Geneviève suddenly let herself go and started weeping, but so quietly and wearily that her tears seemed to lull her to sleep.

'I'll leave you alone with her, madame. I think she should rest while you wait for the doctor. In my opinion – and I swear that I have unfortunately seen a fair number of cases of this kind – the danger is past.'

Naud's voice could be heard on the telephone:

'Right away, yes . . . My daughter . . . I'll explain . . . No . . . Come as you are, in your dressing gown, it doesn't matter . . .'

As he passed Naud, Maigret took a letter the man was holding out of his hand. He had seen it on the girl's bedside table but hadn't had time to grab it.

'What are you doing?' Naud exclaimed, hanging up the telephone. 'That's to me and her mother . . .'

'I'll give it back to you in a moment . . . Go up to her.'
'But . . .'

'I assure you your place is there.'

As for him, he went into the drawing room and carefully closed the door. He was holding the letter in his hand, in two minds as to whether to open it.

'Well, Groult?'

'You don't have the right to arrest me.'

'I know . . .'

'I haven't done anything illegal . . .'

That outrageous statement almost earned him another slap, but Maigret would have had to cross the drawing room to give it to him and he didn't have the strength.

He toyed with the letter, hesitating to tear open the purple envelope. Eventually he did.

'Is that letter addressed to you?' Groult protested.

'Not to me, or to you . . . Geneviève wrote it when she was about to take her life . . . Do you want me to give it back to her parents?'

Dear Mama, dear Papa,
I love you, please believe that, I beg you. But I have to go away for ever. There's nothing else I can do. Don't try to find out why and, most of all, never let Alban into this house again. He . . .

'Tell me, Cavre. While we were upstairs, did he tell you everything?'

Maigret was sure that, in his panic, Alban would have confessed out of a need to cling to someone, to have someone on his side. Who better than a man whose job it was, and whom he would only have to pay?

As Cavre bowed his head, Maigret added:

'What do you reckon, eh?'

Groult, his cowardice knowing no bounds, protested, 'She was the one who started it . . .'

'I suppose she was the one who gave you dirty little books to read?'

'I never gave her any . . .'

'You didn't show her any of the etchings I spotted in your library either?'

'She found them when I had my back turned . . .'

'And no doubt you felt the need to explain them?'

'I'm not the first man of my age to have had a young girl as a mistress . . . I didn't force her . . . She was very much in love . . .'

Maigret laughed insultingly, looking the fellow up and down.

'It was her idea to call Retailleau too, was it?'

'Admit it: if she took another lover, that's none of my business. I think you've got a nerve blaming me for that! Just now, in front of my friend Naud . . .'

'What did you say?'

'In front of Naud, if you prefer, I didn't dare reply. You had the upper hand . . .'

A car stopped by the porch. Maigret went to open the door and said, as if he was the master of the house, 'Quick, go up to Geneviève's room . . .'

Then he went back into the drawing room, still holding her letter in his hand.

'It was you, Groult, who were seized with panic when she told you she was pregnant. You are a coward. You have always been a coward. Life scares you so much you don't dare live it yourself, you have to worm your way into other people's lives . . .

'Groult was going to palm off that child on some fool who'd take responsibility for being the father . . .

'It's so convenient! . . . A young man is seduced and believes himself to be genuinely loved . . . Then one fine day he is told that his embraces have had repercussions . . . All he has to do is go and see Papa, get down on bended knee, beg forgiveness and declare himself willing to make up for it . . . Meanwhile you'd have carried on as the lover, eh?'

'Bastard!'

It was a little thing Pockmarks had said that had put him on the trail:

Albert was furious . . . He knocked back a few brandies one after the other before he went to see her . . .

Then there was the young man's attitude towards Geneviève's father. He had been insolent. He had used the filthiest language to talk about Geneviève.

'How did he find out?'

'I don't know . . .'

'Would you rather I go and ask the girl?'

Groult shrugged. What difference did it make anyway? They couldn't do anything to him.

'Retailleau went to the post office every morning to pick up his employer's post while it was being sorted. He used to go behind the counter. Sometimes he'd help with the sorting. He recognized Geneviève's handwriting on a letter she had written to me because she hadn't been able to see me in private for a few days.'

'I understand . . .'

'Apart from that, everything was working out fine. And if you hadn't interfered . . .'

Of course Albert was furious when he set off that night, with the famous letter in his pocket, to break it off with the girl who had deceived him. And how could he not have believed they had all conspired to delude him, including her parents?

They had put on an act for him. And they still were. Now the father was just pretending to catch him to force him to marry her . . .

'How did you know that he had intercepted the letter?'

'I went to the post office soon afterwards. The postmistress said, "Oh, I think there's a letter for you."'

'She looked but couldn't find it. I telephoned Geneviève. I asked the postmistress who was there when the post was being sorted and then I realized. I . . .'

'You sensed things were going wrong and felt the need to go and see your friend, the prefect's private secretary, in La Roche . . .'

'That's my business . . .'

'What do you reckon, Justin?'

But the latter refrained from answering. They heard heavy footsteps on the stairs. The door opened. Étienne Naud appeared, morose and exhausted, his large eyes full of questions he was trying vainly to answer. Maigret had the letter in his hand, and just at that moment he dropped it so clumsily that it landed on the logs and immediately caught fire.

'What are you doing?'

'I'm sorry . . . Not that it matters, of course, because

your daughter is safe and she'll be able to tell you what was in the letter herself . . .'

Was Naud fooled? Or was he like one of those patients who senses he's being told a lie, who only half-believes the doctor's optimistic words, or doesn't even believe them at all, but begs to hear them all the same, such is his need for reassurance?

'She's better, isn't she?'

'She's asleep. It seems as if the danger is past thanks to your quick response. Thank you from the bottom of my heart, inspector . . .'

The poor fellow looked lost in the drawing room, as if it were a piece of clothing that had grown too big for him. He eyed the bottle of Armagnac and almost poured himself a glass, but a sense of propriety restrained him. Maigret had to pour him one and one for himself.

'To your daughter's health and to an end to all these misunderstandings . . .'

Naud looked up at him wide-eyed with surprise. 'Misunderstandings' was the last word he expected to hear.

'We have been chatting while you were upstairs. I think your friend Groult has something very important to tell you. Believe it or not, he has entered into divorce proceedings without telling anyone.'

Naud looked bewildered.

'Yes. He has other plans. You may not be particularly thrilled by it all. Not to break is better than to mend, I know, but it's a start . . . Come on then! I'm asleep on my feet . . . Didn't someone say earlier that there's a train in the morning?'

166

'At eleven minutes past six . . .' Cavre put in. 'Incidentally I think I'll take that one . . .'

'Well then, we'll travel together . . . In the meantime I'm going to lie down for a couple of hours . . .'

He couldn't help stopping in front of Alban and saying flatly, 'A dirty trick!'

It was still foggy. Maigret had forbidden anyone to accompany him to the station, and Étienne Naud had respected his wishes.

'I don't know how to thank you, inspector. I haven't behaved well towards you . . .'

'You have made me feel very welcome, and I have enjoyed some excellent meals at your table.'

'You'll tell my brother-in-law . . .'

'Of course! . . . Ah, a piece of advice, if I may . . . About your daughter . . . Don't put her through the mill . . .'

A weak, fatherly smile showed Maigret that Naud had understood, perhaps more than he might have suspected.

'You are a very decent sort, inspector. Very, very decent! . . . My gratitude . . .'

'Your gratitude will last to your dying breath, as one of my friends used to say . . . Goodbye. Send me a little postcard now and then . . .'

He left behind him the light on the façade of the house, which otherwise seemed asleep. Only two or three plumes of smoke rose from the village's chimneys and merged with the fog. Looking like a factory from a distance, the dairy was working at full capacity, while old Désiré was steering his boat full of milk churns along the canal.

No doubt Madame Retailleau was in bed, and the little postmistress, and Josaphat, sleeping off his drink, and . . .

Up until the last minute, Maigret was afraid of running into Louis Pockmarks. He had put so much faith in him. Soon no doubt, when he found out he'd left, he would say bitterly:

'*He was one of them too!*'

Or:

'*They got him!*'

If *they* had got him, it wasn't with money, at least, or fine words.

As he waited for the train at the end of the platform, keeping an eye on his suitcase, Maigret talked to himself:

'You see, son, I'm like you, I'm also one of those people who wishes everything was beautiful and pristine on earth . . . I feel hurt and outraged too when . . .'

Ah, look! Cavre had appeared and was standing fifty metres from the inspector.

'Take that character there. He's a bad lot. A devious trick hasn't been invented that he wouldn't stoop to. I am speaking from experience. But I still feel a little sorry for him. I know him. I know what he's worth and what he goes through . . . What good would it have done getting Étienne Naud convicted? Would he have been convicted, for a start? There's no evidence against him. The case would have stirred up so much dirt. Geneviève would have been put on the stand. As for Alban, he wouldn't even have come to the police's attention. The truth is, he would have been delighted to be relieved of his responsibilities . . .'

There was no sign of Pockmarks. It was for the best. Despite everything, Maigret didn't feel proud of himself. Leaving in the early morning like this felt a bit like running away.

'You'll understand later . . . *They* are strong, as you said . . . *They* stick up for each other . . .'

Justin Cavre had seen Maigret and come over, but didn't dare speak to him.

'You hear that, Cavre? I'm talking to myself like an old man.'

'Do you have any news?'

'News of what? The girl's fine. The father and mother . . . I don't like you, Cavre. I pity you, but I don't like you. It's one of those things. There are some animals you feel drawn to and others you don't . . . But, between you and me, I'll tell you something . . . There is one expression I consider the most repellent in the whole language, from the highest to the most humble – every time I hear it it makes me start and sets my teeth on edge. Do you know what it is?'

'No.'

'Everything will work out fine!'

The train was pulling in. Amid the growing din, Maigret shouted:

'Well, you'll see, everything will work out fine . . .'

Two years later, as a matter of fact, he happened to hear that Alban Groult-Cotelle had got married to Mademoiselle Geneviève Naud in Argentina, where her father had set up a large cattle ranch.

'Too bad for our friend Albert, eh, Louis? There's always got to be some poor fellow who carries the can for everyone else!'

INSPECTOR MAIGRET

OTHER TITLES IN THE SERIES